James Loch

Dates and Documents relating to the Family and Property of Sutherland

Anatiposi

James Loch

Dates and Documents relating to the Family and Property of Sutherland

Reprint of the original.

1st Edition 2023 | ISBN: 978-3-38230-796-7

Anatiposi Verlag is an imprint of Outlook Verlagsgesellschaft mbH.

Verlag (Publisher): Outlook Verlag GmbH, Zeilweg 44, 60439 Frankfurt, Deutschland
Vertretungsberechtigt (Authorized to represent): E. Roepke, Zeilweg 44, 60439 Frankfurt, Deutschland
Druck (Print): Books on Demand GmbH, In de Tarpen 42, 22848 Norderstedt, Deutschland

DATES AND DOCUMENTS

RELATING TO THE

FAMILY AND PROPERTY

OF

SUTHERLAND,

EXTRACTED CHIEFLY

FROM THE ORIGINALS

IN THE

CHARTER ROOM AT DUNROBIN.

BY THE LATE

JAMES LOCH, ESQ.

NOT PUBLISHED.

1859.

I.—DATES CONNECTED WITH THE EARLY HISTORY OF SUTHERLAND.

A.D. 940.
990. } MAGBROGDUS, Thane of Sutherland, "who was come "from DUNROBIN, encamped, with his ally LIOTUS, "in the central dales of Caithness." (Cordiner, p. 135.)

A.D. 1009.
1020. } "Alaine, Thane of Sutherland, defeated the Nor-"wegians." (Cordiner, p. 143.)

A.D. 1031. "Alaine Sontherland, Thane of Sontherland, over-"threw the Danes at Drumlea, near Creigh." (Sir Rob. Gordon, p. 23.)

A.D. 1061. Walter Southerland, Thane of Sontherland, created Erle of Southerland by King Malcolm III., and "from this Walter, the Erles of Southerland do "lineally descend, and do continue successively, "without interruption of blood, unto this day." (Sir Rob. Gordon, pp. 23, 24.)

A.D. 1194.
1214. } Hugo Freskyn

(See Sutherland case. Preface to the Registrum Episcopatus Moraviensis.)

II.—CHARTERS CONNECTED WITH GRANTS OF REGALITIES AND THE GENERAL TITLES OF THE EARLDOM.

1601.
April 29. Charter by James the Sixth, in favour of John (6) Earl of Sutherland, by which the Charter of Regality, granted by David the Second in favour of his nephew, William (3) Earl of Sutherland, and dated at Lanerk 10th November, 1345, was confirmed and extended by the annexation of Strathnaver, Edderachylles and Durness and other lands, to the Earldom and Regality of Sutherland, by the erection of Brora into a Burgh

B

of Regality, and by the creation of the hereditary Sheriffdom of Sutherland.

Jacobus Dei gratia Rex Scotorum omnibus probis hominibus totius terre sue clericis et laicis Salutem. SCIATIS nos dedisse, concessisse et disposuisse tenoreque presentis carte nostre dare, concedere et disponere predilecto nostro consanguineo Joanni Sutherlandie comiti suisque heredibus masculis inter ipsum et dominam Annam Elphingstoun Sutherlandie comitissam ejus sponsam legitime procreatis seu procreandis ;

Quibus deficientibus suis heredibus masculis de corpore suo legitime procreandis ;

Quibus deficientibus Roberto Gordoun suo fratri germano suisque heredibus masculis de corpore suo legitime procreandis ;

Quibus deficientibus Alexandro Gordoun etiam suo fratri germano suisque heredibus masculis de corpore suo legitime procreandis ;

Quibus omnibus deficientibus Adamo Gordoun filio legitimo Georgii Marchionis de Huntlie, suisque heredibus masculis quibuscunque hereditarie ;

Totum et integrum comitatum de Sutherland, ac omnes et singulas terras ejusdem comitatus cum castro de Dwnrobene ;

Ac cum annexis connexis dependentiis tenentibus tenandriis libere tenentium servitiis lie outsettis molendinis piscariis, tam in aquis salsis quam dulcibus, advocationibus et donationibus ecclesiarum et capellaniarum earundem et omnibus suis pertinentiis jacentibus infra vicecomitatum nostrum de Innernes.

QUIQUIDEM comitatus ac terre ejusdem cum castro predicto ac aliis supraspecificatis perprius dicto nostro charissimo consanguineo Joanni Sutherlandie comiti perprius hereditarie pertinuerunt, et per ipsum suosque procuratores ad hoc legitime constitutos et literas suas patentes in manibus nostris tanquam in manibus domini sui superioris earundem sursum reddite pureque et simpliciter per fustum et baculum apud Dalkeith resignate fuerunt, ac totum jus et clameum proprietatem et possessionem que seu quas in eisdem habuit habet seu quovismodo habere vel clamare potuit omnino quieteclamavit imperpetuum, Pro hac nostra nova carta et infeodatione dicto nostro charissimo consanguineo Joanni Sutherlandie comiti suisque heredibus masculis et tallie respective et successive prescriptis modo inferius specificato, nostro sub magno sigillo

desuper in debita forma danda et conficienda. NEC NON dedimus
concessimus et disposuimus tenoreque presentis carte nostre
damus concedimus et disponimus prefato nostro charissimo consanguineo Joanni Sutherlandie comiti suisque heredibus masculis et
tallie respective et successive predictis hereditarie

    totam et integram unam davatam terre de

Knokfyn

     unam davatam terre de

Fre.

     unam davatam terre de

Swyisgill

     unam davatam terre de

Kynbrasche

     duas davatas terre de

Kyldona

     duas davatas terre de

Dwyboill

     unam davatam terre de

Balnavaleach

     ac unam davatam terre de

Helmisdaill

    cum pendiculis ejusdem nuncupatis

Achaadaleyis

    et earundem pertinentiis ;

 QUEQUIDEM terre predicte perprius unam partem comitatus
Sutherlandie extiterunt ac per predicessores dicti Joannis Sutherlandie comitis comitibus de Caithnes pro tempore alienate fuerunt
et per charissimum nostrum consanguineum Georgium nunc comitem de Caithnes suosque procuratores ad hoc legitime constitutos,
et literas suas patentes in manibus nostris tanquam in manibus
domini sui superioris earundem sursum reddite pureque et simpliciter apud Dalkeyth per fustum et baculum resignate fuerunt ac
cum omnibus jure et titulo proprietate et possessione que seu
quas in eisdem habuit habet vel quovismodo habere vel clamare
potuit omnino quieteclamavit imperpetuum in favorem dicti nostri
charissimi consanguinei Joannis Sutherlandie comitis ejusque
heredum masculorum et tallie predictorum pro hac nostra nova
carta et infeodatione ipsis desuper in debita forma danda et
conficienda.

Ac ETIAM dedimus concessimus et disposuimus tenoreque presentis carte nostre damus concedimus et disponimus dicto nostro charissimo consanguineo Joanni Sutherlandie comiti suisque heredibus masculis et tallie predictis hereditarie

Totas et integras terras et baroniam de

Far

  cum aquis et salmonum piscariis earundem,

     terras de

Armedaill

Straith

       cum aquis et salmonum piscariis earundem

Renew

Kynnald

Golspetor

Delreid

Cattak

Broniche

Killicalumkill

Dawache Lochnavir

Dawache Eriboill

     duas denariatas terre in

Strone

    insulam de

Sanda, videlicet tres denariatas terre ibidem

    insulam de

Haga, extendentem ad duas denariatas terre

     terras de

Millines et

Hoip

      cum aquis et salmonum piscariis earundem.

Galdwell

Balnahacles

Skelpik

Mowadell

Mekill Grub

Littill Grub

Syrecarnoch

Innernaver

Thorisdaill

      cum aquis et salmonum piscariis earundem.

Mekill Borge
Littill Borge
Kirkboyll
Tung
Skrabister
Kennysyde
Candloch
Edderdawachellis
        aquam de
Torrisdaill
        cum salmonum piscariis earundem
Awchynes
Clybrek
Langall
Rosuall
Raygill
Ardnedell
Skarre
Letterlyoll
Letter-wyndeschoir
Ardnaboill
Houndland
Strathoridall
——— insulam de
       molendina de
Tong
Far, et
Kynnald
  cum multuris et lie suckin eorundem

  cum castris, turribus, fortaliciis, maneriebus, molendinis, multuris, sylvis, parcis, piscariis tam in aquis salsis quam dulcibus, advocationibus et donationibus beneficiorum, tenentibus, tenandriis, libere tenentium servitiis et omnibus earundem pertinentiis, jacentibus in Straythnavarne infra vicecomitatum nostrum de Innernes predictum. QUEQUIDEM terre et baronia cum aliis prescriptis et pertinentiis perprius prefato nostro charissimo consanguineo Joanni Sutherlandie comiti hereditarie pertinuerunt et quas ipse per procuratores suos ad hoc legitime constitutos et literas suas patentes in manibus nostris tanquam in manibus domini sui superioris earundem apud Dalkeyth sursum reddidit pureque et simpliciter per fustum et baculum resignavit ac totum jus et clameum proprietatem et possessionem que seu quas in eisdem habuit habet vel quovismodo habere vel clamare potuit omnino quieteclamavit imperpetuum. Ad hunc effectum ut nos easdem ad comitatum Sutherlandie antedictum modo infra scripto annecte- mus in debita et competenti forma ut congruit.

INSUPER nos pro bono fideli et gratuito servitio nobis per pre- fatum nostrum charissimum consanguineum Joannem Suther- landie comitem prestito et impenso de novo anexavimus et incor- poravimus tenoreque presentis carte nostre pro nobis et succes- soribus nostris annexamus et incorporamus prefatam unam davatam terre de Knokfyn—prefatam davatam terre de Fre— prefatam davatam terre de Swyisgill—prefatam davatam terre de Kynbrasche—prefatas duas davatas terras terre de Kyldona—pre- fatas duas davatas terre de Dwyboill—prefatam davatam terre de Balnavaleache ac dictam davatam terre de Helmisdaill cum pendi- culis ejusdem nuncupatis Achaadaleis et omnibus earundem perti- nentiis quibuscunque iterum ad predictum comitatum Sutherlandie cum eodem inseparabiliter pro perpetuo omni tempore affuturo remanendas, tanquam unam partem et pertinentem dicti comitatus. ET SIMILITER nos ex certa scientia et proprio motu pro diversis magnis respectibus nos moventibus etiam annexavimus et incor- poravimus tenoreque presentis carte nostre pro nobis et successo- ribus nostris annexamus et incorporamus Totas et integras predictas terras et Baroniam de Far cum aquis et piscariis earundem—pre- dictas terras de Armadaill—Straith cum aquis et piscariis earundem —Renew—Kynnauld—Golspetor—Delreid—Cattach —Broniche — Killicalumkill—Davach Loch Naver—Davach Eriboill—duas denariatas terre in Strone—Insulam de Sanda, viz., tres denariatas terre ibidem—Insulam de Haga, extendentem ad duas denariatas terre—dictas terras de Millenes et Hoip cum aquis et piscariis ejusdem. Galdwall—Balnahacles — Skelpik—Mowadell—Mekill Grub—Littill Grub —Syrecarnoch—Innernaver—Thorisdaill cum aquis et piscariis earundem—Mekill Borge— Littill Borge—Kirk- boill — Tung — Scrabister — Kennysyde—Candloch—Edderda- wachellis—aquam de Torrisdaill cum piscariis ejusdem—Awchy- nes—Clybrek — Langoill — Rosuall — Raygill — Ardnedell— Skarre— Lettirlioll — Lettir-wyndeschoir— Ardnaboill—Hound-

land—Strathoridall—Insulam de ———— Molendina de Tung
Far et Kynnald cum multuris et lie sucken earundem, ac cum omnibus castris, turribus, fortaliciis, molendinis, sylvis, piscariis, advocationibus et donationibus beneficiorum, tenentium, tenandriis, libere
tenentium serviciis et omnibus earundem pertinentiis AD predictum
Comitatum Sutherlandie cum eodem inseparabiliter tanquam unam
propriam partem et pertinentem ejusdem comitatus Sutherlandie
pro perpetuo omni tempore futuro remanendam. PRETEREA nos
de novo dedimus concessimus et disposuimus tenoreque presentis
carte nostre damus concedimus, et disponimus prefato nostro charissimo consanguineo Joanni Sutherlandie comiti suisque heredibus
masculis et tallie predictis hereditarie. Totum et integrum predictum comitatum Sutherlandie ac omnes et singulas alias terras
predictas ad ejusdem comitatum annexatas et incorporatas ut premissum est cum castris, turribus, fortaliciis, molendinis, sylvis,
piscariis, carbonibus, carbonariis, salinis, patellis, annexis, connexis, dependentiis annexatisque pertinentiis, advocationibus, donationibus beneficiorum, tenentibus, tenandriis, libereque tenentium
serviciis et earundem omnibus pertinentiis una cum omnibus, jure,
titulo, interesse, jurisclameo, tam petitorio quam possessorio, que
seu quas nos nostri predecessores aut successores ad easdem seu
ad aliquam earundem partem habuimus, habemus, seu quovismodo
habere vel clamare poterimus, aut poterint vel ad census firmas aut
devorias earundem de quibuscunque annis vel terminis preteritis
ratione warde relevii nonintroitus estchaete forisfacture recogni-
tionis, purprusionis, disclamationis bastardie, infeofamentorum,
sasinarum, seu retornatorum reductionis totius aut majoris partis
alienationis aut ob quamcumque aliam causam seu occasionem pre-
teritam diem date presentem precedentem renunciando et exone-
rando eisdem cum omnibus actione et instantia earundem pro
nobis et successoribus nostris prefato nostro charissimo, consanguineo Joanni Sutherlandie comiti suisque heredibus masculis et
tallie predictis pro nunc et in perpetuum cum pacto de non petendo
ac cum supplemento omnium defectuum tam nominatorum quam
non nominatorum, quos tanquam pro expressis in hac presenti
carta nostra haberi volumus.

INSUPER nos perfecte intelligentes per inspectionem nostrorum
antiquorum registrorum necnon per inspectionem veterum infeofamentorum per nostros nobilissimos progenitores, concessorum

predecessoribus dicti Joannis Sutherlaudie comitis et presertim
per quondam Davidem regem Scottie nobilissime memorie quod
antedictus comitatus Sutherlandie per prefatum Davidem regem
Scottie et alios suos excellentissimos progenitores, concessus et
dispositus fuit ad predecessores dicti nostri charissimi consanguinei
Joannis Sutherlandie comitis in unam liberam regalitatem pro
perpetuo tenendam adeo libere, cum omnibus privilegiis et immunitatibus unius libere regalitatis sicuti aliqua alia regalitas infra
regnum Scottie. IDEO ac pro diversis aliis magnis respectibus et
bonis considerationibus nos moventibus Nos ex certa scientia et
propria motu, EREXIMUS, creavimus, univimus, anexavimus, et
incorporavimus tenoreque presentis carte nostre pro nobis et successoribus nostris erigimus creamus unimus, anexamus, et incorporamus integrum predictum comitatum Sutherlandie cum omnibus
et singulis predictis terris baroniis ac aliis supraexpressatis nunc
ad eundem annexatis et incorporatis ut premissum est cum castris,
turribus, fortaliciis, molendinis, sylvis, piscariis, annexis, connexis,
dependentiis, advocationibus et donationibus beneficiorum, tenentibus, tenandriis, libere tenentium servitiis et omnibus earundem
pertinentiis quibuscunque. IN UNAM INTEGRAM et liberam regalitatem cum libera capella et cancellaria cum omnibus et singulis
privilegiis, immunitatibus, jurisdictionibus, casualitatibus, proficiis
et commodatibus quibuscunque ad unam liberam Regalitatem cum
libera capella et cancellaria spectantibus et pertinentibus prefato
nostro charissimo consanguineo Johanni Sutherlandie Comiti suis
que heredibus masculis et tallie predictis hereditarie pro perpetuo
omni tempore affuturo per ipsos possidendam—gaudendam et uten-
dam adeo libere in omnibus respectibus sicuti aliquis alius dominus Regalitatis iufra hoc nostrum regnum. AC ETIAM intelligentes
prefatum nostrum charissimum consanguineum Joannem Sutherlandie comitem eo animo exstare magnos sumptus et expensas im-
pendere pro domorum constructione et edificatione ac pro policia
super lie Inverdebruray jacentem infra dictum comitatum Sutherlandie pro nostrorum liegiorum ac aliorum extraneorum ibidem
frequentantium magno commodo et asiamento Ideo nos bonam
intentionem dicti nostri charissimi consanguinei collaudantes ad
commoditatem reipublice nostri regni tendentem, Ereximus, fecimus constituimus et creavimus tenoreque presentis carte nostre
pro nobis et successoribus nostris erigimus, facimus constituimus et

creamus dictum lie Inver de bruray, terras toftas croftas lie ontsettis
cum omnibus particulis pendiculis et earundem pertinentiis, IN
UNUM liberum burgum baronie et regalitatis prefato nostro charissimo consanguineo Joanni Sutherlandie comiti suisque heredibus
masculis et tallie antedictis burgum de Innerbroray omni tempore
affuturo nuncupandum, Cum speciali et plena potestate prefato
nostro charissimo consanguineo suisque heredibus masculis et
tallie predictis, ballivos, consules, burgenses, liberos serjandos ac
omnes alios officiarios necessarios infra predictum burgum pro
ejusdem gubernatione constituendi et eligendi et eosdem toties ipsis
videbitur expediens deponendi, imponendi et extraponendi ac cum
speciali et plena potestate burgensibus et liberis dicti burgi ad lie
pak et peill et infra predictum burgum et libertatem ejusdem
emendi et vendendi vinum et ceram, pannum laneum et lineum
latum et strictum, ac omnes alias mercantias et stapule bona, ac
infra predictum burgum tenendi et admittendi pistores brasiatores
laniatores piscium venditores sartores calciarios textores allutarios
scissores carpentarios fabros et omnes alios artifices necessarios
ad liberi burgi libertatem spectantes et pertinentes Ac cum potestate ipsis edificandi et tenendi infra predictum burgum pretorium
et crucem foralem et unum forum hebdominatim die Sabbathi una
cum quatuor liberis nundinis annuatim viz. super diem festi concep-
tionis, sancti petri apostoli, petri advincula et super diem sancti
michaelis Ac cum privilegio forum tenendi ad dictas nundinas
pro spacio duarum dierum et integras custumas earundem colli-
gendi et recipiendi Et easdem pro communi bono dicti burgi ap-
plicandi Et generaliter omnia alia et singula faciendi exercendi et
utendi adeo libere sicuti aliquis alius burgus baronie et regalitatis
infra regnum nostrum.

PRETEREA intelligentes quod terre molendina sylva piscaria et
alia particulariter subtus mentionata quarum una pars jacet infra
bondas Sutherlandie ac alia pars jacet infra bondas de Caithnes
et infra nostrum vicecomitatum de Innernes, omnes dicto nostro
charissimo consanguineo Joanni Sutherlandie comiti in feudiferma
et hereditate pertinentes, et per ipsum suosque predecessores ab
antiquo de episcopo de Caythnes tenentes ante annexationem
terrarum ecclesiasticarum hujus nostri regni ad coronam nostram,
et nunc per ipsum de nobis immediate tenentes virtute acti annexa-
tionis dictarum terrarum ecclesiasticarum hujus regni nostre corone,

Ex quibus nos nostrique successores immediati superiores consti-
tuti sumus, et quod integre terre ac alie subtus specificate dicto
nostro charissimo consanguineo in feudiferma et hereditate spec-
tant et pertinent ut premissum est.

Viz. Omnes et singule terre et ville de

Galdwell

Caldell

Cramnage

Barolye

Slanys

Astlermoir

Astlerbeg

Sandwatt

Tarriagaviss

Crannamannycht

Caruagarrow, cum molendinis et piscariis earundem, et cum
    piscariis de

Laxfurde, et aquis de,

Ardurines, et lie cruvis earundem

Hoa, insula de, cum aliis insulis ibidem et piscariis earundem.

Kilmale Kirktoun, terre de, cum pendiculis earundem nun-
    cupatis.

Auchnacalzie.

Stambuster, terre de

Brymmes, terre dimietatis de

Fors, terre de, cum molendinis et piscariis earundum

Baillie, terre de

Lythmoir, due partes terrarum de

Lythmoir cum duabus denariatis terrarum tertie partis de,

Owist, due partes terrarum de

Dorarie, et

Myrremichaellis, terre de,
    novem denariate terrarum cum dimidia denariate terre de

Scrabister, cum lie castel wairdis et langrig de Scrabister,
    et piscariis earundem cum lie sklaitheuch et halkes in

Hoburneheid et pertinentiis.

Weik et Papigo, decem denariate terre de, cum croftis nun-
    cupatis

Bischopisquoyis, Kenzeochisquoyis cum aliis croftis ibidem
    et tenementis in

Villa de Weik, et superiorate earundem terre de
South Kilmister,
North Kilmister, cum molendino de
Wyndles, et pertinentiis
Myreland moir, tres lie ottonis landis in; et pertinentiis, cum
    decimis garbalibus integrarum predictarum terrarum
Mekill Ullagrahame, terre de
Littell Ullagrahame
Halkrig, cum molendinis, piscariis et lie cruvis earundem
Westerdaill, terre de
Esterdaill
Thornesdaill
    cum quarta parte salmonum piscarie iu aqua de
Thurso.
Subanister, denariata terre de
Diran, terre de
Alterwell, cum lacu earundem
Staustell, tres denariate cum dimidia denariate terre de,
Skebomanys terre de, cum pendiculis nuncupatis
Braymort
Skebo, orientalis pars de
Wester Skebo, terre de, et
Skebo Castell
Ulleste, terre de
Ardaleis
Airthvaiche, cum pendiculis nuncupatis
Airthgormeta, et
Airthnicholas
Sythera terre de, cum crofta nuncupata
Tayclyb
Davochfyn terre de.
Drumdewan et
Ferrytun de Portnicoulter cum pertinentiis, molendinum de
Skebo cum croftis et tenementis infra civitatem de Dornoch
Palatium de Dornoch cum le assyiss aill et thoill dicte civitatis
    usitata et consueta cum superiorate ejusdem
Brymmes, tredecim denariate cum dimidia denariate terre de
Rogarmoir terre de, cum molendino et pertinentiis
Skail, terre de, et
   Regeboill ;

cum tenentibus tenandriis libere tenentium serviciis omnium et singularum terrarum ac aliarum supra specificatarum cum pertinentiis una cum hereditariis officiis constabularie castrorum et palatiorum de Skrabister Skebo et Dornoch ac de hereditario officio Balliatus integrarum predictarum terrarum cum omnibus feodis privilegiis et devoriis eorundem.

ET NOS CONSIDERANTES quod inhabitantes, infra terras et bondas predictas eorum habitationes procul a quocunque legitimo ordinario judicio seu justicio secundo habentes, pauperes ibidem habitantes quotidie oppressi sunt pro nunc justicie administratione inter ipsos, et destituti existentes ex ordinarii judicii consolatione inter ipsos residentis infra dictas bondas, nullum remedium seu ordo cum oppressoribus capitur, ad magnum nostri animi merorem. PRO cujusquidem opportuno remedio nos ex auctoritate nostra regali, et regia potestate, EREXIMUS creavimus et incorporavimus omnes et singulas predictas terras, molendina, sylvas, piscarias ac alias particulariter et generaliter supra expressatas, jacentes infra bondas respective predictas cum omnibus earundem partibus pendiculis et pertinentiis quibuscunque, prefato nostro charissimo consanguineo Joanni Sutherlandie comiti. spectantibus et pertinentibus ut premissum est hereditarie: IN UNUM severalem et distinctum vicecomitatum et jurisdictionem per se, vicecomitatum Sutherlandie omni tempore affuturo nuncupandum, et antedictum burgum de Innerbroray capitalem burgum antedicti vicecomitatus ordinandum, et fecimus constituimus et ordinavimus tenoreque presenti carte nostre pro nobis et successoribus nostris facimus constituimus et ordinamus prefatum nostrum charissimum Joannem Sutherlandie Comitem suosque heredes masculos et tallie antedictos hereditarios vicecomites antedicti vicecomitatus Sutherlandie. AC ETIAM hereditarios coronatores ejusdem vicecomitatus super integras bondas et terras predictas ac dedimus concessimus et disposuimus tenoreque presentis carte nostre damus, concedimus et disponimus hereditaria officia antedicta, vicecomitatus et coronatoris infra integras bondas et terras predictas in hujusmodi vicecomitatu incorporatas cum omnibus feodis privilegiis jurisdictionibus et immunitatibus casualitatibus proficiis et devoriis quibuscunque ad predicta officia Vicecomitis et Coronatoris quovismodo spectantibus et pertinentibus, prefato nostro charissimo consanguineo Joanni Sutherlandie Comiti heredibus

masculis et tallie predictis pro nunc et in perpetuum cum speciali et
plena potestate suisque ipsis eorumque deputatis et officiariis dicta
officia antedicti vicecomitatus et coronatoris respective antedicti
vicecomitatus infra integras terras et bondas predictas cum omnibus
jurisdictionibus privilegiis et immunitatibus ejusdem utendi et
exercendi adeo libere in omnibus respectibus, sicuti aliquis alius
hereditarius Vicecomes seu Coronator infra regnum nostrum facit
seu facere possit. NEC NON volumus et concedimus ac pro nobis
et nostris successoribus pro perpetuo decernimus et ordinamus
quod unica sasina nunc per prefatum nostrum charissimum con-
siliarium Joannem Sutherlandie Comitem ac omni tempore
affuturo per suos heredes masculos et tallie predictos apud
predictum Castrum de Dwnrobene capienda, stabit et ipsis
erit sufficiens sasina pro toto et integro predicto comitatu et regalitate Sutherlandie ac pro omnibus et singulis terris ejusdem
Comitatus et Regalitatis cum dicto Castro de Dwnrobene et
omnibus et singulis et aliis terris castris, turribus, fortaliciis, maneriebus, domibus, edificiis, hortis, pomariis, carbonibus, carbonariis,
salinis, patellis, columbariis, molendinis, terris molendinariis, multuris, sylvis, parcis, forrestis, nemoribus, piscariis, tam in aquis
salsis quam dulcibus, toftis, croftis, lie outsettis, lacubus, aquis,
annexis connexis, dependenciis, partibus, pendiculis, advocationibus, donationibus, et juribus patronatum ecclesiarum, beneficiorum capellaniarum earundem, cum tenentibus, tenandriis, libere
tenentium serviciis et omnibus suis pertinentiis, Ac pro antedicto
burgo baronie et regalitatis de Innerbroray cum integris privilegiis et immunitatibus ejusdem, omnes nunc in unam liberam
regalitatem cum libera capella et cancellaria erectos ut premissum est, ac etiam predictis hereditariis officiis vicecomitis
et coronatoris Sutherlandie infra integras terras et bondas supra
expressatas cum feodis casualitatibus, jurisdictionibus et privilegiis
earundem quibuscunque, non obstante quod non jacent insimul et
contigue sed in diversis partibus super quibus nos pro nobis et successoribus nostris dispensavimus ac per presentes dispensamus pro
nunc et in perpetuum. TENENDUM ET HABENDUM totum et integrum predictum comitatum et regalitatem Sutherlandie ac omnes et
singulas terras ejusdem Comitatus et Regalitatis cum antedicto
Castro de Dwnrobene et omnes et singulas alias terras cum castro,
turribus, fortaliciis, maneriebus, domiciliis, edificiis, pomariis,

hortis, carbonibus, carbonariis, patelis, salinis, columbariis, molendinis, terris molendinariis, multuris, sylvis, parcis, forestis, nemo ribns, piscariis, tam in aquis salsis quam in dulcibus, toftis, croftis lie outsettis, lacubus, aquis, annexis, connexis, dependentiis, partibus, pendiculis, advocationibus, donationibus et juribus patronatum ecclesiarum capellaniarum et beneficiorum, cum tenentibus, tenandriis, libere tenentium servitiis et omnibus earumdem pertinentiis Ac cum· dicto burgo baronie et regalitatis de Inverbroray privilegiis et immunitatibus ejusdem omnes nunc in unam liberam regalitatem cum libera capella et cancellaria erectos ut dictum est Ac etiam antedicta hereditaria officia Vicecomitis et Coronatoris antedicti vicecomitatus Sutherlandie infra integras terras et bondas supra expressatas nunc in unum severalem et distinctum vicecomitatum per se erectum ut premissum est, cum omnibus feodis casualitatibus jurisdictionibus, privilegiis, et immunitatibus earundem ac ad ejusdem officia Vicecomitatis et Coronatoris spectantibus et pertinentibus prefato nostro charissimo consanguineo Joanni Sutherlandie comiti suisque heredibus masculis et tallie respective et successive expressatis. De nobis et successoribus nostris in feodo hereditate ac libero comitatu et regalitate ac libero burgo in baronia et regalitate cum libera capella et cancellaria ac in libero severali et distincto vicecomitatu per se antedictum vicecomitatum Sutherlandie nuncupandum pro nunc et imperpetuum per omnes rectas metas suas antiquas et divisas prout jacent in longitudine et latitudine, In domibus, edificiis, boscis, planis, moris, maresiis, viis, semitis, aquis, stagnis, rivolis, pratis, pascuis, et pasturis, molendinis, multuris et eorum sequelis, aucupationibus, venationibus, piscationibus, petariis, turbariis, carbonibus, carbonariis, cuniculis, cuniculariis, columbis, columbariis, fabrilibus, brasinis, bruariis et genestis, sylvis, nemoribus et virgultis, lignis, tignis, lapidiciis, lapide et calce Cum curiis et earundem exitibus, herezeldis, bludewitis et mulierum merchetis, cum communi pastura libero introitu et exitu Ac cum furca, fossa, sok, sak, tholl, thame, wert, wrak, ware, vennyson, infangthief outfangthief, pit et gallous ac cum omnibus aliis et singulis libertatibus, commoditatibus, propriis asiamentis ac justis suis pertinentiis quibuscunque tam nominatis quam non nominatis tam subtus terra quam supra terram, procul et prope ad predictum comitatum, baronias, terras, officia, regalitatem aliaque antedicta cum suis pertinentiis, spectantibus, seu juste spectare valentibus, quomodo libet in futurum libere, quiete, plenarie, integre, honorifice, bene et in pace absque ulla revocatioue, contradictione, impedimento aut obstaculo quocunque.

REDDENDO annuatim prefatus noster charissimus consanguineus Joannes Sutherlandie Comes suique heredes masculi et tallie predicti nobis et successoribus nostris pro antedicto comitatu et regalitate unum par calcarium deauratorum in die festi Joannis baptiste nomine albe firme si petantur tantum, et hoc ex nostra scientia et proprio motu non obstante quod antedictus comitatus perprius per prefatum nostrum charissimum consanguineum suosque predecessores de nobis et nostris nobilissimis progenitoribus per servitium warde et relevii tenebatur. Quod nos pro diversis magnis respectibus nos moventibus in alba firma pro nobis et successoribus nostris permutavimus ac per presentis carte tenorem permutamus pro nunc et in perpetuum Ac pro antedictis hereditariis officiis vicecomitis et coronatoris antedicti vicecomitatus Sutherlandie infra integras terras et bondas predictas prefatus noster charissimus consanguineus Joannes Sutherlandie comes suique heredes masculi et tallie predicti faciendo et administrando justiciam per seipsos eorumque deputatos et officiarios in predictis officiis respective ut de jure congruit. Necnon reddendo nobis et successoribus nostris unum par calcarium deauratorum annuatim in die festi Joannis Baptiste nomine albe firme si petantur tantum. IN CUJUS REI testimonium huic presenti carte nostre magnum sigillum nostrum apponere precipimus TESTIBUS predilectis nostris consanguineis et consiliariis Joanne Marchione de Hamiltoun, comite Arranie, domino Evan, etc. Joanne comite de Montrois, domino Grahame, etc. Cancellario nostro. Georgio Mariscalli comite, domino Keyth, etc. regni nostri marescallo. dilectis nostris familiaribus conciliariis dominis Jacobo Elphinstoun de Barnetoun nostro secretario, Ricardo Cokburne juniore de Clerkingtoun nostri secreti sigilli custode, militibus. Magistro Joanne Skene nostrorum rotulorum registri ac consilii clerico, domino Joanne Cokburne de Ormestoune milite, nostre justiciarie clerico, et magistro Willielmo Scott de Grangemure nostre cancellarie directore. Apud Dalkeyth penultimo die mensis Aprilis anno domini millesimo sexcentissimo primo regnique nostri anno trecesimo quarto.

Contract between King Charles I. and John Earl of Sutherland,
for the resignation of the Regality of Sutherland.

1631.
July 18.
Aug. 26.

CHARLES R. At Oatlands and Halyrudhous respectively the auchteene day of July and twenty six day of August, the zeir of God One thousand six hundred and threttie-ane zeiris. It is appointed, agriet, finallie contractit and endit betwix the most excellent heich and michtie Prince and Monarche Charles, be the Grace of God, King of Scotland, Ingland, France and Ireland, defendar of the Faith, and with advyse and consent of His Majestie's richt traist Cousigne and Counsallour Williame Erle of Mortoun, Lord Dalkeith and Aberdour, and Heiche Thesaurer, Comptroller, and Collectour-Generall of His Majestie's new augmentationnis within the kingdome of Scotland, and of His Majestie's traist Cousigne and Counsallour Johne Lord Stewart of Traquair, and His Majestie's Deput in the saidis offices, and also with advyse and consent of the Lordis and utheris of His Majestie's secreit Counsal and Excheker of the said kingdome of Scotland on the ane pairt, and His Majestie's right traiste Cousigne Johne Erle of Sutherland, Lord Strathnaver, on the uther pairt, in maner, forme, and effect as aftir followis :—That is to say, FOR SA MEKILL as umquhile Johne Erle of Sutherland, father to the said Johne now Erle of Southerland, was heritablie infeft and seaset be Chartour and Infeftment, grantit to him under the great Seall by his Majestie's umquhile darrest father King James the Sext of worthie and eternall memorie off the dait, the penult day off Apryll, the zeir of God 1601 zeiris, and Instrument of Seasing following thereupone, adittit the   day of   , In all and haill the richt and privieledge of Regalitie within the haill boundis off the Erledome off Sutherland, in maner at lenth mentionat and contenit in the said Infeftment lykeas umquhile King David the Secund, His Majestie's predecessour of worthie memorie be his Chartour and Infeftment of the dait at Lanerk, the tent day of October, and seventene zeir of his reyne, gave grantit and confirmet to umquhile Williame Erle of Sutherland, and to His Majestie's sister Margaret spous to the said Erle, and to thair airis, to be gotten betuix thame (of quhome the said Johne, now Erle of Sutherland is lineallie discendit) the said Erledome of Sutherland in ane frie regalitie for ever with all liberties, commodities, easmentis, and

richteous pertinentis which are knawn to perteine to ane frie regalitie as amplie and surelie as any regalitie within the said kingdome
of Scotland is bruikit and possest, and sicklyke for sa meikle
as the said umquhile Johne Erle of Sutherland, be vertue of the
forsaid Chartour and Infeftment grantit be His Majesties said
umquhile darrest father of the dait forsaid, and Seasing following
thereupone, wes heritablie infeft in all and haill the heretable office
of Scherifschip of the Scherifdome of Sutherland comprehending
the boundis and limitis specifiet in the said infeftment. Lykeas be
the said Infeftment the said umquhile Erle and his airis, mail
and of taillie specifiet and contenit therein, are maid and creat not
onlie heretable Schereffis of the said Scherifdome, but also heretable Crowneris of the samyn Scherifdome, and in the saide Char-
touris and Infeftmentis of the daitis respectively above writtin at
mair lenth is contenit, AND als forsamekill as the said Johne,
now Erle of Sutherland wes upone the seventene day of Apryll,
the zeir of God 1617 zeirs dewlie and lawfullie infeft and senset as
air to the said umquhile Johne Erle of Sutherland, that last
deceaset his father, In all and haill the said richt and privieledge
of frie regalitie within the haill boundis of the said Erledome of
Sutherland, with the haill privieledges, liberties, commodities, easmentis, and richteous pertinentis of the samyn, And also in all and
haill the saidis heretable offices of Scherefschip and Crownerie of
the said Scherefdome of Sutherland with the haill liberties, privieledges, and immunities of the samyn within the haill boundis
thereof, as the said Infeftment of the dait forsaid at mair lenth
purports. AND His Majestie being fullie resolvet to have all the
heretable offices and jurisdictionnis within this kingdome drawen
and reducet to the Crowne and prerogative royall in the maist easie,
just, and commodious way, and His Majestie upone some offeris
and overtouris maid be the said Johne now Erle of Sutherland,
for surrandering of the saidis heretable offices in His Majestie's
handis for ane reasonabill satisfactioun having remittet the consi-
deratioun thereof to the Commissionaris of Surranderis and Teynds,
They be thair Act of the dait the 17 day of Junij, the zeir of
God 1631 zeiris, have fund the saidis offeris and overtouris reasonabill in thameselves, and according thairto ordanet His Majestie's
Advocat to draw up ane perfyke and formale resignatioun of the
saidis offices and richtis of Regalitie, Scherifschip, and Crownerie

D

to be subscrybet be the said Erle, togidder with suche writtis and securities as may secure the said Erle in the possessioun of the saidis richtis and offices untill the compositioun and summe aftir specifiet extending to the summe of Ane thousand punds sterling, be reallie and trewlie payit be His Majestie to the said Erle, hes airis, Executors, or Assignayis, THAIRFORE the said Johne now Erle of Sutherland, for obedience and fulfilling of his pairt of the said Act, binds and obleissis him and his forsaidis to resigne, renunce, surrander, and overgive fra him and his forsaidis, in the hands of His Majestie and His Hienes' successourris, and in thair favour all and haill the said heretable richt and titill of Regalitie, togidder with the saidis heretable offices of Scherifschip and Crownerie of all and haill the said Scherifdome of Sutherland, with the haill fees, privieledges, liberties, commodities, and immunities perteining and belonging thairto, togidder with all and sundrie chartours, preceptis, seasingis, infeftmentis, and other richtis, titillis, and securities quhatsoevir maid and grantit to the said Erle, his predecessours and authoris, or conceivet in thair favour be quhatsumevir persoun or persounes of and concerning the said heretable richt and titill of Regality forsaid, and of the saidis heretable offices of Sherefschip and Crownerie, liberties, privieledges, and casualties perteining thayrto, togidder with all richt, titill, interest, clame of richt, propertie, and possessioun, petitory, and possessory, actioun and instance which the said Erle or his forsaidis had, hes, or ony wayis may have clame or pretend thairto, or to ony pairt thairof, in time cuming, reserving allenarlie to the said Erle and his forsaidis, the libertie and privieledge of Baronn Courtis, pit and gallous, with the jurisdictioun of Baronie, liberties and privieledges of the samyn within so manie of the landis, baronies, Erledome and Schereffdome forsaid, quhilk the said Erle and his successours holdis, or sall hold of His Majestie, and His Hienes' successours in frie Baronie, and no further, and for the better denuding of the said Erle and his forsaidis of the heretable richt and titill of regalitie and heretable offices of Schereffschip and Crownerie abovespecifiet with the privieledges and casualities perteining thairto, the said Erle hes maid, constituted, and ordanet, and by the tenor heirof, makis, constitutes, and ordaines James Douglas maister to the secreit counsell and Exchekker, and ilk ane of thame conjunctlie and severallie,

the said Johne Erle of Sutherland, his verie lawful, undoubtit
and irrevocable procurators, actors, factors, aud speciall earand
bearers to the effect underwrettin, gevin, grantand, and committand to thame, and ilk ane of tham conjunctlie and severallie, as
said is, his verie full, frie, plaine power, generall and speciall command, express bidding, mandat, and chairge for him in his name,
and upone his behalff to compeir befor Our Soverane Lord and
His Hienes' successours immediat lawful superiours of the said
richt of Regalitie, offices of Scherifschip and Crownerie above specifiet, or before thair Commissionaris, quhatsumever day or
dayis, place or places, lawful and convenient, and thair with all
dew reverence and humilitie as becumes purelie and simplie be staff
and bastoune as use is To resigne, renounce, surrander, overgive,
and delyver fra the said Erle, his airis and successours, lykeas the
said Johne Erle of Sutherland be the tenor heirof resignes, re-
nounces, surranders, overgives, and delyvers fra him and his forsaids, all and haill the said heretable richt and titill of Regalitie
of all and haill the said Erledome of Sutherland, and haill lands,
baronies, and utheris perteining and annexed thairto, with the
pertinents, togidder with the said heretable offices of Scherifschip
and Crownerie of all and haill the forsaid Scherifdome of Sutherland, with the haill free privieledges, liberties, commodities, immunities, casualities, and dewties perteining and belonging thairto,
togidder with all richt, titill, intres, clame of richt, propertie,
and possessioun, petitorie, and possessorie quhilk the said Erle or
his forsaids had, hes, or onywayis may have, ask, clame, or pretend thairto, or to ony pairt thairof in tyme cuming IN THE HANDIS
of our said Soverane Lord or His Hienes' successours, or thair
Commissionaris forsaid, or in the handis of the said Erle, his immediat, lawfull superiours of the samyn. IN FAVOURIE of His Majestie,
and His Hienes' successours forsaidis ad perpetuam remanentiam
To remaine with thame for ever Reserving allenarlie to the said
Erle and his forsaidis, the libertie and privieledge of Baronn Courtis,
pit and gallous, with the jurisdictioune of Baronie liberties and
privieledges of the samyn within so many of the landis, baronies,
Erledome and Scherifdome forsaid quhilk the said Erle and his
successours holds, or sall hold, of His Majestie and His Hienes's
successours, in frie baronie, and no further actis, instrumentis, and
documentis, ane or mo thairupone, to ask, lift, and raise, And ge-

nerallie all and sundrie uther thingis to do, use, and execute anent
the premissis siclyke, and as friely in all respectis as the said Erle
micht do thairin himselff if he were personallie present, promittend
to hold firme and stabill all and quhatsumever thingis his said procuratours or ony of thame conjunctlie and severallie in his name in
the premissis richteouslie dois, Quhilk surrander and resignatioun
the said Erle binds and obleissis him and his forsaids to warrand,
acquyet, and defend, to be guid, valid, effectuall, and sufficient in
the selff, fra his awin and his forsaids proper factis and deedis and
fra the proper factis and deedis of his predecessours, Erles of
Sutherland allenarlie AND His Majestie, with consent forsaid, willis
and declaris that efter the payment of the said summe of Ane
thousand pundis sterling, efterspecifiet, quhilk is appoynted to be
payit to the said Erle and his forsaids for the pryce and compositioun of the surrander of the forsaidis heretable richtis and
offices, that the said richt and titill of regalitie sall be supprest and
extinguished for ever With the haill privieledges, liberties, commodities, and casualities perteining and belonging thairto; But as
to the said jurisdictioun of Scherifschip and Crownerie his Majestie
willis and declairis that the samyn sall be onlie supprest and extinguished in swa far as the samyn are heretable, but not in swa far
as the samyn are severall jurisdictiouns and offices necessar for
the governement and peace of the Kingdome, quhilk his Majestie
willis and declairis to stand in the awin force and effect with the
lyke privieledges and liberties as perteines to ony uther Scherifdome
of this Kingdome not being heretable, AND farder, His Majestie
considering how necessar it is that the said Countie of Sutherland, togidder with the landis efter following, lying maist ewest
and contigue thairto be of new established in ane haill and frie
Scherifdome, to be governet be thair awin Scheriffis and uther
officiaris requisit to that effect. THAIRFORE His Majestie with
advyse and consent of the saidis Lordis and utheris of His Hienes'
secreit counsall and exchekker of this said kingdome, HES of new
erected and incorporat, and by the tenor herof of new erectis and
incorporatis, all and haill the said countrie of Sutherland with the
countries of Strathnaver, Assint and Fairniecostar, alias Sleischeles,
with the haill boundis, landis, baronies, erledomes, Lordschips,
waters, fischingis, mylnes, and utheris, within the samyn. IN ANE
HAILL, frie, severall and distinct Scherifdome be the selff To be

callit now and in all tyme cuming, the Scherifdome of Sutherland
to be governet by the Scheriffis and utheris officiaris perteining to
the jurisdictioun of ane Scherifdome in all tyme cuming. Lykeas
His Majestie with advyse and consent forsaid of certaine knowledge and proper motive, disunits, dissolvis, and dividis the said
landis and countries of Assint and Fairniecostar alias Sleischeles
quhilk for the present ar ane pairt of the Scherifdome of Innerness
in respect of the far distance thairof fra the Burghe of Innerness
quhilk is the heid Burghe of the said Scherifdome of Innerness, and
unites, annexis, and incorporatis the saidis Landis and Countries of
Assint and Fairniecostar alias Sleischeles, with the haill boundis of
the samyn To the said Scherifdome of Sutherland, in respect of the
neirnes and contiguitie thairto, and commodiousnes of the samyn.
Lykeas His Majestie with consent forsaid of certaine knowledge and
proper motive for His Hienes and his successours, willis and ordaines that the said Scherifdome of Sutherland comprehending the
haill lands and boundis quhilk of before perteinet to the said Scherifdome of Sutherland, and are exprest in the said Infeftment grantit
be his Majestie's said umquhile darrest Father to the said umquhile
Johne last Erle of Sutherland in the moneth of Apryl, 1601 zeiris
Togidder with the saidis landis and countries of Assint and Fairniecostar now addit thairto sall be and remaine ane severall and distinct Scherifdome be the selfe seperat frome the said Scherifdome
of Innernes in all tymecuming within the boundis and limitis efter
following, vizt. Begynnand upone the northe at the strype callit
Faehallodaill quhilk devydis Strathnaver from Caithnes, and fra
that south-east be the topis of the hillis to the Ord upone the
sey-coste, including the haill boundis of the Orde, and thairfra
south-west till the mouthe of the water of Tayne alias Portnacuter, and fra that west till the water of Oikell, comprehending
thairin the haill landis and countrie of Fairniecostar alias Sleischeles, and fra that west till Lochbrome and Coygache swa far as the
dyocis of Caithnes extendis, comprehending thairin the saidis landis
and countrie of Assint unto the west sey, and fra thence northe
up the seycoste till the northmest poynt of the land called Ardurienes, and fra thence east to the river and water of Hallodaille,
and fra that east to the said strype called Faehallodaill ; AND His
Majestie willis and declaris, and for His Hienes and his successours with advyse and consent foresaid, decernes and ordanes that

the heid burghe of the said Scherifdome of Sutherland is, and sall
be the toune and burghe of Durnoche, laitlie erected be His Majestie's selff, in ane frie burghe royall, and that all proclamatiouns
and executiouns of breves, horneingis, inhibitiounis, denuncia-
tiounes, weaponnschowingis, and utheris of the lyke nature, swa far
as concernes the haill inhabitantis within the said Scherifdome of
Sutherland within the haill boundis and limitis of the samyn aboveexprest, sall be uset, and execute at the Mercat Croce, and in
the said Burghe of Durnoche, and that all services of brieves and
registratiounnis of the said horneingis, inhibitionnis, and uthiris
forsaids sall be uset and maid within the said toune and burghe of
Durnoche, as the heid burghe of the said Scherifdome, and that
the Scheriffis for the tyme, their Clerkis and Deputs sall hald
thair Courtis within the said burghe, and be resident thairin for
that effect, AND His Majestie with advyse and consent forsaid be the
tenor herof geves and grantis full power, libertie, and licence to
the frie baronns and utheris inhabitantis, within the said Scherifdome of Sutherland now present, and to thair successours in all
tyme cuming, to elect, appoynt, nominat, and chose thair awin
Commissionaris for the said Scherifdome of Sutherland to compeir
for thame, and in thair names at all Parliamentis, meetingis, and
generall conventionnis within this kingdome for the publick ef-
fairis of the samyn at all occasiounis requisit and necessar as
effeirs, and they to have thair vote thairin, and the samyn to be
as effectuall as the vote of ony utheris Commissionaris of ony
uther frie Scherifdome within this kingdome, AND His Majestie be
the tenor herof, in verbo principis for His Hienes and his successours with advyse and consent forsaid, doth faithfullie promeis
to ratifie, approve, and confirme this present contract in the haill
heids and articles thairof; togidder with the erectioun and unioun
above specifiet of the forsaid Scherifdome within the haill boundis
and limitis of the samyn aboveexprest liberties and privieledges
thairof, and of the forsaid burghe royall liberties and privieledges
perteining thairto, and exprest heirintil, and in the Chartour and
Infeftment thairof forsaid grantit thereanent, and that in His
Hienes' Hiche Court of Parliament nixt to be halden within the
kingdome of Scotland for the whiche thir presentis sall be ane
sufficient warrand to the Lordis of Articles of the said Parliament
to that effect, ATTOUR His Majestie with advyse and consent for-

said faithfullie promitis and obleissis him and His Hienes' successours to content and pay to the said Johne Erle of Sutherland and his forsaidis, as for the pryce and compositioun of the surrander abovespecifiet, all and haill the summe of Ane thousand punds sterling, extending to the summe of Twelff thousand punds scottis usuall money, quhilk is appointet to be payit by His Majestie and His Hienes' successours at sik tyme as they sall think fit and expedient, and that the said Erle and his forsaidis sall bruik and possess the forsaidis richtis and offices of Regalitie, Scherifschip, and Crownerie, be virtue of the wodsett underwrittin, ay and quhill the said summe of ane thousand punds sterling be compleitlie payit to the said Johne Erle of Sutherland or his forsaidis in maner following, AND THAIRFORE His Majestie with advyse and consent foresaid, hes agreit and condiscendit to impignorat and wodset Lykeas His Majestie be the tenor heirof, with advyse and consent foresaid, impignorats and wodsettis to the said Johne Erle of Sutherland, his airis mail and assignayis quhatsumever, all and haill the said richt of Regalitie of all and haill the said Erledome of Sutherland, and offices of Scherifschip and Crownerie above specifiet of the said Scherifdome of Sutherland within the haill boundis and limittis of the samyn above exprest, unit, annext, erected, and incorporat in maner abovementionat with all and sundry fies, privieledges, jurisdictiounes, immunities, casualities, proffeitis, and deuties quhatsumever perteining or belonging to the saidis richtis and offices of regalitie, Scherifschip and Crownerie in maner abovewrittin. To be halden of His Majestie and his hienes' successours in maner and for payment of the blenche deutie efter specifiet, under reversioun, alwayis be payment of the said somme of Ane thousand punds sterling in maner efterspecifiet, AND His Majestie with advyse and consent forsaid faithfullie promeissis to infeft and sease the said Johne Erle of Sutherland and his foresaidis, in all and haill the said richt of regalitie of the said Erledome of Sutherland, and haill landis, baronies, and utheris perteining to the said Erledome, quhairin the said Erle and his predecessours had the richt of regalitie of before. Togidder with the haill privieledges, liberties, immunities, and casualities perteining to the said regalitie, and to erect the said Erledome, and haill landis, baronies, and utheris perteining thairto in frie regalitie with frie chapell and chancellarie, as amplie and frielie as the said Erle and his predecessours had and bruikit the samyn of before. To be halden of His Majestie and his Hienes' successours in frie blenche for payment of ane penny upon the ground of the said regalitie, or ony pairt thairof zeirlie at the feast of Witsonday, in name of blenche ferme if it be askit allanerlie, redemable alwayis and under reversioun in maner following and siclyke, to infeft and seise the said Erle and his forsaidis, in all and haill the heretable offices of Scherifschip and Crownerie of the said Scherifdome, within the haill boundis and limittis thairof above exprest, comprehending the haill landis, baronies, and utheris lyand within the said Scherifdome erectit of before. Togidder with the said landis of Assint and Fairnie-costar now addit thairto, with the haill frie commodities, privie-ledges, immunities and casualities perteining to the samyn To be halden of His Majestie and his Hienes' successours in frie blenche for payment of ane penny upone the ground of ony pairt of the said Scherifdome zeirlie at the feast of Witsonday, in name of blenche ferme, if it be askit allanerlie dureing the not redemp-tioun of the samyn be vertue of the reversioun underwrittin, redim-able alwayis and under reversioune, Lykeas, it is heirby expresslie provydit and declairit that the forsaid richt of regalitie and of-fices of Scherifschip and Crownerie sall be redimable to His Majestie and his successonrs in maner eftir following, viz., That quhensoever it sall please his sacred Majestie and his succes-sours or thair Thesaurers in His Majestie's name to content and pay to the said Johne Erle of Sutherland his airis, executours, or assignayis all and haill the said somme of Ane thousand pundis ster-ling, extending to the said somme of Twelff thousand punds Scottis money, haveand course of payment for the tyme within the great kirk of Edinburghe, callit Sanct Goillis Kirk, at that pairt thairof whare the tombe of umquhile James Erle of Murray is situat, upone the premonitioun of fourtie dayis wairneing to be maid before any terme of Witsonday or Martimas, to the said Erle or his for-saids personallie, or at thair dwelling places, being for the tyme in presence of ane notar and witnesses as effeiris, and in caice of refuiss, or not compeirance to the ressait of the said somme the samyn to be consignet in the handis of the Deane of Gild or Theasaurer of the said Burghe of Edinburghe, being for the tyme, To be furthcum-and to the said Erle and his forsaidis ; That than, and in that caice, the said Johne Erle of Sutherland and his forsaids sall be bund and obleist Lykeas, the said Erle be the tenor heirof bindis and obleissis him and his forsaids to resigne, renounce, surrander, overgive, and denud himselff and his foresaidis omni habili modo of the haill richt and titill of the foresaidis richtis and offices of Regalitie, Scheriffschip, and Crownerie, with the haill free privieledges, liberties, commodities, immunities, casualities, profeits, and deuties quhatsumever perteining and belonging thairto. Togidder with all and sundrie Chartours, Preceptis, Infeftmentis, Seasingis, Richtis, Titillis, and Securities quhatsumever maid or to be maid and grantit to the said Erle and his foresaidis by His Majestie, thairupon To and in favour of his said sacred Majestie and His Hienes' successours to remaine with thame for ever. Reserveing allanerlie to the said Erle and his foresaidis the libertie and privieledge of baronn courtis, pit, and gallous, with the jurisdictioun of baronie, libertie and privieledges of the samyn, within swa many of the Landis, Baronies, Erledomes and Scherifedome foresaid, quhilk the said Erle and his successours haldis or sall hald of His Majestie and His Hienes' successours in frie Baronie and no further, Provyding alwayis the said Erle be no farther obleist in warrandice of the premissis; but fra his awin and his airis, assignayis, and successours factis and deidis done, or to be done in prejudice of the samyn, and fra the factis and deidis of his predecessours Erles of Sutherland. Lykeas the said Erle, be the tenor heirof bindis and obleissis him and his foresaidis to warrand, acquyet, and defend the forsaid renunciatioun, resignatioun, and dispositioun To be guid, valeid, effectuall, and sufficient in the selff fra the said Erle and his forsaidis proper factis and deidis, and fra the factis and deidis of his said predicessours Erles of Sutherland allanerlie. To wit, that the said Erle nor his foresaids hes not done, nor sall do nothing in prejudice of thir presentis, And for the mair securitie, His Majestie with the consent forsaid, and the said Johne Erle of Sutherland, ar content and consents thir presentis be insert and registrat in the buiks of Counsall and Sessioun, or buiks of Excheker of the said Kingdome of Scotland To have the strenthe of ane Act and Decreit of the Lordis thairof, with all neidful executioun to follow thairupone in forme as effeiris and to that effect constitute

Thair Procuratours and ilk ane of tham conjunctlie and severallie

E

to compeir and consent to the registratioun heirof in maner forsaid, promitteñ de rato. In witnes quhairof (written by Johne
Sempill, servitor to Henrie le Vaitche, wryter to his Majestie's sig-
net) His Majestie hes sealled and suprascryvet and the said Lordis
and utheris of Counsal and Excheker, and the said Johne Erle of
Sutherland, have subscryvet thir presentis with thair handis, day,
moneth, zeir, and place abovewrittin before thir witnessis, Mr.
James Keith, servitour to William Erle of Stratherne and Mon-
teith, President of his Majestie's Privie Counsall and Lord Heiche
Justice of Scotland, Mr. Alexander Burnet, servitour to Sir Thomas
Hope of Craighall, his Majestie's Advocat, Alexander Lyntoun,
wryter in Edinburghe, and Gilbert Gourdoun, servitour to the said
Johne Erle of Sutherland, suprascryvet thus :—Charles R., and
subscryvet thus, Geo. Cancell, Stratherne, Wintoun, Linlithgow,
Sterling, Pa. B. of Ross, Thomas Hope, Arskyne, Elphinstoun,
Scottistarvett, Traquaire, James Baillie, Southerland, H. Raythe,
witness, Alex. Burnet, witnes, Alex. Lyntoun, witnes, Gilbert
Gordoune, witnes.

Signed at Oatlands, the 18 day of July, 1631. Subscryvet
be the Erle of Sutherland, at Halyrudhaus, 26 August, 1631.

Charter in terms of the aforesaid Contract in favour of John
Earl of Sutherland.

1631. } CAROLUS Dei Gratia Magnæ Britannie Francie
Sept. 14th. } et Hibernie Rex Fideique Defensor OMNIBUS probis
hominibus suis ad quos presentes litere pervenerint
salutem SCIATIS Quia per contractum et appunctuamentum
initum et confectum inter nos cum avisamento et consensu principalis nostri thesaurarij et deputati infrascript. nec non dominorum aliorumq. nostri secreti consilij et secretarij regni nostri
Scotie ab una, et predilectum nostrum consanguineum Joannem
comitem de Sutherland ab altera partibus de data apud Oatlands et
Halyrudhous respective decimo octavo die mensis Julij et vigesimo
sexto die mensis Augusti respective anno domini millesimo sexcen-
tesimo trigesimo primo prefatus noster consanguineus Joannes
Sutherlandie comes a semetipso heredibus suis et assignatis quibuscunq. Resignavit renunciavit et extra-donavit Totum et integrum

hereditarium jus et privilegium Regalitatis infra integras bondas
Sutherlandie comitatus Prout in dicto contractu continetur una
cum hereditarijs officijs vicecomitis et coronatoris totius et inte-
gri Sutherlandie vicecomitatus infra integras bondas et limites
ejusdem cum omnibus feodis privilegijs libertatibus commoditatibus immunitatibus casualitatibus et divorijs ad predictum hereditarium jus Regalitatis hereditaria officia Vicecomitis et Coronatoris
infra bondas dict. Regalitatis et Vicecomitatus spectan. et pertinen.
una cum omni jure et titulo que dictus comes suiq. predicti habuerunt habent seu quovismodo ad eadem aut aliquam earundem
partem pretendere poterint in futurum. In manibus nostris et in
nostro nostrorumq. successorum favore ad perpetuam remanentiam
RESERVATIS tamen dicto nostro consanguineo suisq. predictis libertate et privilegio baronie curiarum et lie pitt et gallous cum jurisdictione baronie libertatibus et privilegijs ejusdem infra totidem
terras baronias comitatum et vicecomitatum predictum quot
dictus comes suiq. successores de nobis et nostris successo·ibus
tenet seu tenebunt in libera baronia et non amplius PRO quaquidem
resignatione nos virtute dicti contractus tenemur solvere prefato
nostro consanguineo Joanni Sutherlandie comiti heredibus suis
masculis aut assignatis quibuscunq. summam mille librarum
sterlingarum lie sterling money extenden. ad summam duodecim
mille librarum monete regni nostri Scotie que per nos aut successores nostros quocunq. tempore nobis vis erit solvi constituitur Et
dictus noster consanguineus suiq. predicti predictum jus Regalitatis gauden. et possiden. infra dictum Sutherlandie comitatum una
cum dictis officijs Vicecomitis et Coronatoris infra dictas bondas
Sutherlandie Vicecomitatus tam ab antiquo eidem spectan. quam
nuper virtute dicti contractus eidem annexat. Idq. semper et donec
dicta summa mille librarum sterlingarum lie sterling sit soluta Et
ad hunc effectum nos cum consensu predicto tenemur dare et
concedere sufficientes cartas et infeofamenta prefato nostro
consanguineo Joanni Sutherlandie comiti suisq. predictis de jure
Regalitatis et officijs Vicecomitatus et Coronatoris predict. Sub
reversione per solutionem dicte summe mille librarum sterlingarum
lie sterling Prout in dicto contractu contineter prout dictus contractus hac in parte ejusdem proportat. IGITUR pro perimpletione
dicti contractus hac in parte ejusdem nos cum avisamento et consensu predilecti nostri consanguinei et consiliarij Willielmi comitis

de Mortoun domini Dalkethe et Abirdour principalis nostri
thesaurarij computorum nostrorum rotulatoris collectoris generalis
iufra hoc regnum nostrum Scotie ac fidi nostri consanguinei et
consiliarij Joannis Domini Stewart de Traquair nostri in dictis
officijs deputati ac etiam cum avisamento et consensu reliquorum
dominorum nostri scaccarij dicti regni nostri commissionariorum
nostrorum impignoravimus dedimus et concessimus ac disposuimus
tenoreq. presentis carte nostre impignoramus damus concedimus et
disponimus Prefato nostro consanguineo Joanni Sutherlandie
comiti heredibus suis masculis et assignatis quibuscunq. hereditarie Totum et integrum dictum jus et privilegium libere Regalitatis infra integras bondas Sutherlandie comitatus predict. sicuti in
eodem contractu latius continetur. AC ETIAM impignoravimus dedimus concessimus et disposuimus tenoreq. presentis carte nostre impignoramus damus concedimus et disponimus predicta officia vice
comitis et coronatoris dicti Sutherlandie vicecomitatus comprehenden. integras terras et bondas ab antiquo eidem vicecomitatui
spectan. ac etiam terras et regiones de Assint et Fairniecostarie
alias Slescheles nuper eidem annexat. infra integras bondas et
limites infraspecificat. et in dicto contractu content. viz. Incipien.
super boreale apud torrentem lie strype nuncupat. Faehallodaill
qui dividit Strathnavar a Cathnes Et illinc pergendo versus austrum
ьrientale per cacumina montium ad lie Orde super maris littus
includen. integras bondas de lie Orde Et inde versus austrum occidentale ad orificium aque de Tayne, alias Portnacuter, Et abhinc
versus occiden. ad aquam de Occeil inde comprehenden. terras et
regionem de Fairniecostarie alias Sleischeles Et illinc versus occiden.
ad Lochbroome et Coygache quousq. Catanie diocessis sese extendit.
Iude comprehenden. dictas terras et regionem de Assint ad mare
occidentale Et illiuc pergendo super maris littus versus borealem
finem terre nuncupat. lie Ardurienes et istinc versus orientem ad
fluvium et aquam de Hallodaill Et illinc versus orientem ad predictum torrentem lie strype nuncupat. Faehallodaill Una cum singulis
feodis privilegijs libertatibus commoditatibus immunitatibus et casualitatibus ad predicta jura et officia Regalitatis Vicecomitis et
Coronatoris spectan. et pertinen. infra integras bondas et limites ante
dictos vicecomitatus predicti duran. non redemptione eorundem
virtute reversionis supra et infraspecificate IN SUPER nos pro causis
suprascriptis DE NOVO univimus annexavimus ereximus et incor-

poravimus Tenoreq. presentis carte nostre cum consensu prescript
de novo unimus annexamus erigimus et incorporamus Totum et integrum dictum Sutherlandie comitatum et singulas terras aliaq.
perprius eidem pertinen. et annexat. In unam integram et liberam
regalitatem cum libera capella et cancellaria cum omnibus et
singulis privilegijs libertatibus immunitatibus et casualitatibus ad
unam liberam regalitatem cum libera capella et cancellaria infra
regnum nostrum Scotie spectan. seu spectare valen. Prefato nostro
consanguineo suisq predictis per ipsos adeo libere in omnibus
respectibus gauden. et possiden. sicuti aliquis alius dominus regalitatis ejusmodi jus privilegium et jurisdictionem regalitatis gaudet et
possidet infra hoc regnum nostrum Idq. semper et donec legitima
redemptione ejusdem virtute reversionis supra et subscripte Post
cujusquidem redemptionem dicta regalitas erectio ejusdem pre-
scripta cum libera capella et cancellaria et jurisdictione ejusdem
cum singulis privilegijs et casualitatibus eidem pertinen. suppressa
dissoluta irrita et extincta erit imperpetuum ac si eadem nunquam
erecta aut in rerum natura exstitisset secundum tenorem dicti
contractus et similiter nos ex certa scientia et proprio motu cum
avisamento et consensu predicto dissolvimus dissunivimus separa-
vimus et dividimus tenoreq. pñtium dissolvimus disunimus separa-
mus et dividimus dictas terras et regiones de Assint et Fairniecostarie alias Sleischeles et integras earundem bondas a vice
comitatu de Innerness ad quem eedem perprius pertinuerunt
Respectu longe ab eodem distantie Et univimus annexavimus ad-
didimus et incorporavimus tenoreq. pñtis carte nostre unimus annexamus addimus et incorporamus Predictas terras et regiones de
Assint et Fairniecostarie alias Sleischeles et integras earundem
bondas ad prefatum Sutherlandie Vicecomitatum Ratione eidem
contiguitatis et propinquitatis cum eodem inseparabiliter tanquam
unam partem et pertinen. prefati Sutherlandie vicecomitatus pro
perpetuo omni tempore affuturo remanen. Ac de novo ereximus et
incorporavimus tenoreq. pñtis carte nostre cum consensu predicto
de novo erigimus et incorporamus Totam et integram dictam
Sutherlandie regionem cum regionibus de Strathnaver Assint et
Fairniecostarie alias Sleischelles cum integris bondis terris baronijs
regionibus dominijs aquis piscationibus molendinis alijsq. infra
bondas et limites eorundem supra express : In unum generalem
et distinctum Vicecomitatum per se nunc et omni tempore affu-

turo Vicecomitatum Sutherlandie nuncupand. per vicecomites aliosq. officiarios ad jurisdictionem vicecomitatus omni tempore affuturo gubernand. Ac dedimus concessimus et disposuimus tenoreq pūtis carte nostre damus concedimus et disponimus hereditarium jus regalitatis predicte cum hereditarijs officijs Vicecomitis et coronatoris infra dictum Sutherlandie vicecomitatum nunc ut premissum est erect. Prefato nostro consanguineo Joanni Sutherlandie comiti suisq. predictis et hoc durañ non redemptione eorundem tantummodo secundum clausulam et conditionem reversionis in dicto contractu mentionat. PRETEREA volumus et concedimus ac pronobis et successoribus nostris cum avisamento et consensu predicto determinimus et ordinamus, Quod villa et oppidum de Durnoche nuper in libero burgo regio lie brugh royall erect. Est et erit capitale burgum dicti Sutherlandie vicecomitatus Et quod omnes proclamationes breviumq. exequtiones cornuationes inhibitiones denunciationes armorum lustrationes lie weaponn schawingis aliaq. ejusmodi nature quatenus ad singulos inhabitantes infra dictum Sutherlandie vicecomitatum attinet infra integras bondas et limites ejusdem supra express. modo ut supra erect. et incorporat. utentur et fungentur apud crucem foralem dicti burgi nostri de Durnoche Et quod omnia brevium deservitia et registrationes dictarum cornuationum inhibitiouem aliorumq. prescriptorium utentur et fierent infra villam et burgum de Durnoche tanquam capitale burgum dicti vicecomitatus Et quod vicecomites ejusdem protempore existeñ eorum clerici et deputati curias suas tenebunt infra dictum nostrum burgum Et ad hunc effectum in eodem versentur. Ac nos cum avisamento et consensu predicto dedimus et concessimus tenoreq. pūtis carte nostre damus et concedimus plenam potestatem libertatem et licentiam liberis baronibus alijsq. inhabitantibus infra dictum Sutherlandie vice comitatum nunc pñtibus eorumq. successoribus omni tempore affuturo eligere substituere nominare et constituere suos commissionarios pro dicto vicecomitatu ad comparandum pro semetipsis et in eorum nominibus ad omnia parliamenta conventus et generalia comitia infra hoc regnum nostrum propter publica negotia ejusdem omnibus occasionibus necessarijs uti congruit Illi vero in ijsdem votum habere et idem tam esse sufficiens quam votum quorumcunq. aliorum commissionariorum cujuscunq. liberi vicecomitatus infra hoc regnum nostrum TENENDUM ET HABENDUM

totum et integrum predictum jus regalitatis dicte Sutherlandie
comitatus et infra singulas bondas terras baronias aliaq. ad dictum
comitatum spectan. in quibus prefatus noster consanguineus
Joannes Sutherlandie comes suiq. predicessores jus regalitatis perprius habuerunt nunc in libera regalitate cum libera capella et
cancellaria erect. una cum antedictis hereditarijs officijs Vicecomitis et Coronatoris dicte Sutherlandie vicecomitatus infra integras
terras et bondas ejusdem supraexpressas Nunc in unum liberum
generalem et distinctum vicecomitatum per se ut premissum est
erect. cum omnibus privilegijs libertatibus feodis immunitatibus et
casualitatibus ad eadem jura et officia regalitatis vicecomitis et coronatoris spectan. et pertinen. Prefato nostro consanguineo Joanni
Sutherlandie comiti heredibus suis masculis et assignatis predictis de nobis successoribus nostris In libera albafirma hereditate
et libera regalitate cum libera capella et cancellaria et in libero
generali et distincto vicecomitatu per se nunc et omni tempore
affuturo Sutherlandie vicecomitatum nuncupandum imperpetuum
Per omnes rectas metas suas antiquas et divisas Prout jacent in
longitudine et latitudine, In domibus edificijs boscis planis moris
marresijs vijs semitis aquis stagnis rivolis pratis pascuis et pasturis
molendiuis multuris et eorum sequelis ancupationibus venationibus
piscationibus petarijs turbarijs carbonibus carbonarijs cuniculis cunicularijs columbis columbarijs frabilibus brasinis
bruerijs et genistis silvis nemoribus et virgultis lignis tignis lapicidijs lapide et calce cum curijs et earum exitibus herezeldis
bludwitis et mulierum merchetis cum furca fossa sok sak thole
thame vert wrak wear veth vennisone, infangtheiff outfangtheiff
pitt et gallous, cum communi pastura liberoq. introitu et exitu Ac
cum omnibus alijs et singulis libertatibus commoditatibus profi-
tuis et asiamentis ac justis suis pertineñ quibuscunq. tam non
nominatis quam nominatis tam subtus terra quam supra terram
procul et prope ad predict. jus et hereditaria officia aliaq. respective
prescript. cum pertineñ spectañ seu juste spectare valeñ quomodo
libet in futurum libere quiete plenarie integre honorifice bene et
in pace absq. ulla revocatione aut. obstaculo aliquali REDDENDO
inde annuatim prefatus noster consanguineus Joannes Sutherlandie
comes heredes sui masculi et assignati predicti Nobis et successoribus nostris pro toto et integro antedicto jure Regalitatis cum
privilegijs libertatibus et casualitatibus eidem pertinen. unum
denarium usualis monete regni nostri Scotie annuatim in die festo

Pentecostes super aliqua parte dicte Regalitatis nomine albefirme si petatur tantum AC PRO dictis officijs vicecomitis et Coronatoris cum privilegijs libertatibus et casualitatibus ijsdem pertinen. alterum denarium usualis monete dicti regni nostri Scotie super aliqua parte dicti vice comitatus annuatim ad dictum festum Pentecostes nomine albefirme si petatur tantum Ac etiam prefatus noster consanguineus suiq. predict faciendo et administrando justiciam per semetipsos eorumq. deputatos et officiarios in predictis officijs ut de jure congruit Ac volumus et declaramus proq. nobis et successoribus nostris cum avisamento et consensu predicto decernimus et ordinamus Quod unica sasina per dictum nostrum consanguineum Joannem Sutherlandie comitem heredes suos masculos et assignatos predictos de predicto jure regalitatis capienda apud castrum de Dunrobene quod est precipuum et principale castrum et maneries prefati Sutherlandie comitatus erit bona valida et sufficiens sasina pro dicta regalitate privilegjs libertatibus atque casualitatibus ijdem pertinen. Ac etiam quod unica sasina per dictum nostrum consanguineum Joannem Sutherlandie comitem suosq. predictos de antedictis officijs vice comitis et coronatoris capienda apud crucem foralem de Durnoche quod est capitale burgum predicti vicecomitatus est et erit sufficiens bona et valida sasina pro dictis officijs vicecomitis et coronatoris cum libertatibus privilegijs immunitatibus et casualitatibus ijsdem spectan. et pertinen. SPECIALITER tamen providetur et declaratur per pñtis hujus carte nostre temnore Quod predictum jus regalitatis officia vicecomitis et coronatoris infra bondas et limites supraspecificatos nobis et successoribus nostris redimibilia fuerint per solutionem prefato nostro consanguineo suisq. predictis summe mille librarum sterlingarum lie sterling vel per consignationem ejusdem eorum utilitati secundum clausulam et conditionem reversionis supraspecificate in omnibus mentionat. et content. in antedicto contractu Post cujusquidem reversionis perimpletionem prefatus noster consanguineus suiq predicti tenebuntur et obligabuntur resignare sursum reddere extradonare et semetipsum suosq predictos omni habili modo de omni jure et titulo dicte regalitatis IN FAVOREM nostrum nostrorumq. successorum denudare et eadem cum singulis privilegijs libertatibus et casualitatibus eidem spectan. suppressa et exstincta fore imperpetuum Ac etiam prefatus noster consanguineus suiq predicti semetipsos de dictis officijs vicecomitis et coronatoris cum omnibus feodis privilegijs libertatibus et casualitatibus ijsdem spectan. denudare eademq. in nostrum nostrorumq. successorum favorem resignare ad perpetuam remanentiam Et eadem solum modo suppressa et exstincta fore quatenus hereditaria officia existunt Et non quatenus sunt distincte et severales jurisdictiones et officia necessaria pro gubernatione et regni nostri pace que nos per pñtis carte nostre tenorem ordinamus stare in eorum proprio vigore infra bondas supra expressas cum ejusmodi privilegijs et libertatibus que ad quemcunq. alium vicecomitatum et coronatorem infra hoc regnum nostrum pertinent hereditaria minime existen. RESERVATIS tamen dicto nostro consanguineo suisq. predictis libertate et privilegio baronie curiarum et lie pitt et gallous cum jurisdictione baronie libertatibus et privilegijs ejusdem infra totidem terras baronias comitatum et vicecomitatum predictum quot dictus comes suiq. predicti de nobis et nostris successoribus tenent seu tenebunt in libera baronia et non amplius DENIQUE nos tenore pñtis carte nostre in verbo principis pro nobis et successoribus nostris cum avisamento et consensu predicto fideliter promittimus Ratificare approbare et confirmare predictum contractum et appunctuamentum in omnibus capitibus articulis ejusdem Una cum erectione et unione supraspecificata antedicti vicecomitatus infra integras bondas et limites ejusdem supraexpress. modo ut supra erect. cum libertatibus et privilegijs ejusdem ac predicti burgi regii lie brughe royall cum privilegijs eidem pertinen et hoc in sequenti nostro parliamento infra hoc regnum nostrum Scotie proxime tenand. IN CUJUS REI testimonium hiuc pñti carte nostre magnum sigillum nostrum apponi precepimus TESTIBUS predilectis nostris consanguineis et consiliarijs Jacobo Marchione de Hammiltoun Comite Arranie domino Even et Avandaill, Georgio vicecomite de Duplin Domino Hay de Kinfannis nostro cancellario, Willielmo Mariscallj Comite Domino Kethe regni nostri Mariscallo, Thoma comite de Hadingtoun domino Bynning et Byres nostri secreti sigilli custode, Willielmo vicecomite de Sterling, Domino Alexander de Tullibody nostro secretario principali, dilectis nostris familiaribus consiliarijs Dominis Joanne Hamiltoun de Magdalenis nostrorum rotulorum registri et consilij clerico, Georgio Elphingstoun de Blythswode nostre Justiciarie clerico, et Joanne Scott de Scottistarvett nostre Cancellarie directore militibus Apud Theobaldis decimo quarto die mensis Septembris Anno Domini millesimo Sexcentessimo trigessimo primo Et anno regni nostri septimo.

F

RESIGNATION OF THE SHERIFFSHIP OF STRATH-NAVER BY DONALD LORD RAE IN FAVOUR OF JOHN EARL OF SUTHERLAND.

1632.
March 19.
1633.
Sep. 26.

Att Edinburgh the twentie sex day of September, the zeir of God 1633 zeiris. IN PRESENCE of the Lordis of Counsall, compeirit Mr. Alexander Cumyng, Prŏr. for Donald Lord of Rae, heritabill Schereff underwrittin and gave in the prŏrie. off Resignatioun underwrittin subscryvit with his hand, desyring the same to be insert and registrat in the buikis of Counsall and Sessioun, To have the strenth of ane decreit of the Lordis thairof, et ad futuram rej memoriam, And quilk desyre the saidis Lords thocht reasonabill, and thairfore hes ordanit and ordanis the said Prŏrie. of Resignatioun to be insert and registrat in the saidis Buikis of Counsall ; Decerns the same to have the strenth of ane Decreit, and to remain thairin ad futuram rej memoriam, Quhairof the tenor followis : BE IT KEND till all men be thir presentis that WE DONALD Lord of Rae, heritabill Schereff underwrittin, to have maid, constitut and ordanit, Lykeas be the tennor heirof mak, constituit and ordain Robert Gray of Creiche and ilk ane of them, conjunctlie and severallie my verrie lawfull and irrevocabill procuratours, actours, factours, and speciall earrandbeareris to the effect underwrittin, Givand,grantand, and committand to tham and ilk ane of them my verrie full, frie, plein power, express command, bidding and chairge, to compeir befor ane noble and michtie Earle, Johne Earle of Sutherland and my immediat superior of the office underwrittin, and thair for me and in my name as use is in sic caiss, to resigne, renunce, surrander, simpliciter, upgive and overgive All, and haill my office of Scherifschip within all and sundrie the pairtis and boundis of the landis and countrie of Strathnavar, with the pertinentis and my power for excerccising of the said office within the same, with all richt, tytill, entreis, clame, kyndnes, propertie or possessioun, I, my airis or assignayis had, hes, or ony wayes may pretend to have thairto, In the handis of the said Earle ad perpetuam remanentiam. Lykas be the tennor heirof, I resigne, renunce, surrander simpliciter, upgive and overgive fra me and my foresaidis all and haill the said office of Scherifschip, within all and sundrie the pairtis and boundis foresaidis, with the pertinentis and my power above writtin, With all richt, tytill, entreis, clame, kyndnes, propertie or possessioun, I or my foresaidis had hes or onywayes may pretend to have thairto, In the handis of the said Johne Earle of Sutherland, to remain with him, his airis and successours perpetuallie heirefter, siclyk and als frielie in all respectis, as gif I had nevir had richt thairto, actis, instrumentis and uyʳ documentis, thairupon to ask, crave, uplift, and receave, and generallie all and sindrie uthir thingis to do, haut, use and execute thairanent, that to the office of ane Prōr in sic caices is knawin to appertein, firme and stabill halding, and for to hald all and quhatsumevir thingis my said Prōrs. conjunctlie and severallie in the premissis in my name lawfullie leidis to be done, But revocation Under pain of law ; and for the mair securitie I am content and consentis that thir presentis be insertt and registrat in the Buikis of Counsall and Sessioun of Scotland to have the strenth of ane Decreit of the Lordis thairof, et ad futuram memoriam, and to that effect makis and constitutis Mr. Alexr. Cumyng, Advocatt, conjunctlie and severallie my verie lawfull and irrevocabill prōr Promitteñ de rato. In witnes of the quilk thing (written be Alexander Napar, I have subscryvit thir pñtis at Greinwiche the nyntein daye of Marche, the zeir of God 1632 zeiris) befor thir witnesses Sir William Forbes, Knicht and Barronet, and William Innes of Sansyd, Sic. Subr., D. Reay, W. Forbes, witnes, William Innes, witnes.

Extractum de libro actorum per me Magistrum Alexandrum Hay, Scribam Consilij ac deputatum honorablis viri domini Johannis Hay Ogland militis clerici Rotolorum ac Registri S. D. N. Regis Sub meis signo et subscriptione manualibus.

(Signed)   A. HAY.

Lands comprised in the Entail of the Earldom of Sutherland, dated 4th October, 1705.

ALL and whole the Earldom of Sutherland, all and sundry the lands of the said Earldom, with the Castle of Dunrobine, and with annexes, connexes, dependencies, tenants, tenandries, and services

of free tenants, outsets, milns, fishings as well in salt as fresh
waters, advocationes, donationes and rights of patronage of the
Churches and Chaplainries thereof, and whole pertinents of the
same whatsoever, lying of old within the Sheriffdom of Inverness,
but now of Sutherland, as also all and whole

> The davoch lands of Knockfyne,
> the one davoch land of Fric,
> the one davoch land of Suyisgill,
> the one davoch land of Kindbrash,
> the two davoch lands of Kildonan,
> the two davoch lands of Duyboill,
> one ox gate of Balnaralreach,
> one davoch of Helmesdaill,
> and the pertinents thereof called Achandalies, and all their
> pertinents.

And also all and whole the lands and

> Barony of Farr, with the salmon fishings thereof;
> Armidall,
> Straith with the salmon fishings thereof;
> Renew,
> Kynald
> Golspetor,
> Dalreid,
> Cattoch,
> Bronich,
> Kilcallumkill,
> Dowach Lochnaver,
> Dowach Ereboill,
> the two penny lands of Strone,
> the island of Sanda,
> the three penny lands there,
> the island of Hoya, extending to one two penny land;
> Millienes, the lands of,
> Hoy, with the salmon fishings thereof;
> Galdwell,
> Balnahacles,
> Skelpick,
> Mowadell,
> Meikle groub,

Littil groub,
Syracarnoch,
Invernaver,
Thoirsdell, with the waters and salmon fishings thereof
Meikle borg,
Littel borg ;
Kirkboill,
Toung,
Scrabister,
Kennesyde,
Candloch,
Edderdawachelles,
the water of Thorisdaill, with the salmon fishings thereof ;
Achayness,
Clybreck,
Langall,
Rosswall,
Raygill,
Arnedell,
Skarr,
Letter lyoll,
Letter wynd shoir
Ardnaboill,
Houndland,
Strathoridaill,
    the island of ————
the Milns of Toung, Farr, and Kynald, with the multures
    thereof, and sicklike.
All and whole the Lands and Barony of
Ardurnes,
Caldwall,
Galdwell,
Cranach,
Borarlie,
Slanys,
Elstermuir,
Elsterbeg,
Sandwatt,
Terragavish,

Carnamanoch,

Carnagarrow,

with the waters of Avingarrow and Sandwatt, with the fishings, mills, and kilns thereof;

the island of Hoa, and other islands therewith; the Havening places; in all the lands and islands above recited

Laxfoord, the half of the fishing of the water of

Ardurnes, the whole fishing of the water of

and the cruive fishing thereof, with the whole fishings of the same as well in salt as fresh water, together with the land sheaves of the aforesaid lands in Ardurnes, multures, and sundry pertinents of the same.

And all and sundry the lands

Killmaliekirktoune, with pendicles of

Auchnacalzie and kiln and crofts thereof.

And also all the lands of

Skebomanes, with the pendicles of

Braymort,

Easter Skebo, with the Dovecot lands and mills of the same;

Wester Skebo,

Ullestrie,

Ardalles,

Auchvayche, with the pendicles called

Auchgormelit,

Auchinbolles,

Sythera with Tayklybe,

Davoch fyne,

Drumdevan,

Ferrietoun of Portencoulter and passage thereof;

Miln of Skebo, with the Multures, Miln lands, Crofts, and Kiln thereof.

And all and whole the Palace of Dornoch, with the crofts, acres, and tenements thereof; the town and city of Dornoch, with all houses, biggings, yeards, tofts, crofts, acres, and tenements thereof.

All and whole of the same used and wont the Ward called *Bishop's Ward*, and the lands called Ernoch, with the Mosses

called the Bishopes Moss, and all other Mosses belonging to the
Bishopric of Caithness, with the Miln of Dornoch and Miln Crofts
thereof, with the abstracted multures thereof, &c.;

    Rogartmore, with the miln, miln lands thereof, &c.;
    Skaill,
    Regeboill,
        with the coals and coal heughs of all and sundry islands,
        &c.

And moreover all the lands commonly called
    Chanterfield alias Auchinchanter;
    Deanfield,
    Balleinknock,
    Archdeanfield,
    Clynkirktoun,
        with the teinds thereof respective included, and the whole
        pertinents of the same lying within the Sheriffdom of
        Sutherland and Deanery of Caithness.

1765. May 24. Elizabeth Sutherland declared by the House of Lords to be Countess of Sutherland, (as heir of William, who was Earl of Sutherland in 1275)—afterwards Duchess Countess of Sutherland, married Sept. 4, 1785, George Granville Leveson Gower, Viscount Trentham, afterwards, successively Marquis of Stafford and Duke of Sutherland, K. G. who was descended in the male line from Sir Alan Gower of Stittenham, Sheriff of York at the Conquest—which estate still continues in the family.

Lands in the Marriage Settlement of Geo. G. Viscount Trentham and of Elizabeth Countess of Sutherland.

1785. Sep. 4. ALL and whole the Lands and Barony of Assynt as particularly described in pages 41 and 42

As also all and whole the towns and lands following lying in the Earldom and Sheriffdom of Sutherland,
    Sydra, and Milntown thereof;

Davochfyne, with the sheallings and grassings thereof
lying in parishes of Dornoch and Rogart,

Drumdivan,

Auldbreck, half davoch lands of

Auchfyne,

Tachlybe,

Rhyne, the town and lands of

with the houses, biggins, yeards, tofts, grassings, shealings,
mosses, muirs, and pertinents of the said whole lands
used and wont, together with the ground right and property thereof, hinds, parsonage and vicarage of the
same ;

Rogartmore,

Little Torboll,

Achachinal,

Easwick,

Ferore,

Tulloch,

Achladuich,

Michaelwells,

Croftinegiduche,

and other parts of the estate of Little Torboll, in and
about Dornoch ;

Dalmore.

And also all and whole the lands of the Estate of

Clyne, comprehending

Clyneleish,

Ardachy,

Tarchallum,

Brora, lying to the east side of the water thereof ;

Clyne, Kirkton of

Clyne, Mylnetown of

Clyn, Myln of, with the miln lands and mulltures thereof

Achendavit, the lands of, with their pendicles and pertinents used and wont and taking in new grounds lying
within the Parishes of Clyne and Kildonan and Sheriffdom of Sutherland aforesaid

And also the one davoch of land of Kilfedder beg,
with the shealings, particularly

Pulenarb,
Kulzean,
Fornachinau,
Pitgrudie,
Crof Maddoch,
Gallowhill,
Cambusavie,
Cambusmore.

III.—DATES CONNECTED WITH THE BARONY
OF SKELBO.

Charter by Hugo Freskyn to Magistro Gilbert—Archidiacono
of Moray.

A.D. 1136 to 1211.

Omnibus hominibus et amicis suis, has literas visuris et audituris, HUGO FRESKYN salutem in Domino. Sciant omnes tam presentes quam futuri, me dedisse, concessisse et hac presenti carta mea confirmasse Magistro Gilberto Archidiacono Moravie et illis heredibus de parentela sua quibus ipse dare et concedere voluerit, et heredibus eorum, totam terram meam de SCELBOL in Suthyr-landia et de Fernebucklyn et Inverchyn. et preterea totam terram meam de Suthyrlandia versus occidentem que jacet inter has terras prenominatas et divisas de Ros. Tenendas et habendas sibi et heredibus suis prenominatis in perpetuum, de me et heredibus meis, per rectas divisas suas, in bosco et in plano, in pratis et in pascuis, in stangnis et in molendinis, in moris et maresiis, in ripis et in piscariis et in omnibus justis pertinentiis suis, libere et quiete, plenarie, pacifice et honorifice. Faciendo pro predictis terris servicium unius sagittarii, pro omni exactione, consuetudine, servicio et demanda, ad me et heredes meos spec-tantes. Et adquietando forinsecum servicium Domini Regis quantum ad predictas terras pertinet. Ego vero Hugo Freskyn et heredes mei predictas terras prenominatas predicto Magistro Gil-berto Archidiacono Moravie et illis heredibus et parentela sua

G

quibus ipse dare et concedere voluerit et heredibus eorum contar omnes homines et feminas warantizabimus acquietabimus et defendemus in perpetuum. Hiis testibus, Willielmus frē meo, Andrea frē meo, Waltero Morthach, Hugone Duglas, Freskyno Duglas, Waldevo de Garuiacht, Roberto Camerario, Reginaldo Janitore, Ricardo de Moravia, Archybaldo de Duffus, Angustino de Elgyn, Thoma filio Angustini, Johanne Nigro, Alexandro de Elgyn, et multis aliis.

A.D. 1211 to 1214.

Confirmation of the preceding Charter by William King of Scots.

Witnesses: Willelmo de Boseho, Cancellario meo, Olivero et Willelmo capellanis meis, Philippo de Valoniis, Camerario meo, Hugone de Sigillo, clerico meo, apud Seleschirk, xxix. die Aprilis.

A.D. 1235.

William de Sutherland confirms the Charter of his father Hugo Freskyn.

Witnesses: Henrico decano de Ros, Mauricio Cancellario, Hugone Duglas, Freskyno de Duglas, Reginaldo Janitore, Johanni nigro et multis aliis.

A.D. 1235, Dec. 26th.

Confirmation by Alexander II. King of Scots, of Charter by Gilbert Bishop of Caithness, formerly Archdeacon of Moray, in favour of Richard Moray, his brother.

Alexander II. dei Gratia Rex Scottorum. Omnibus probis hominibus tocius terræ salutem. Sciant presentes et futuri nos concessisse et hac carta nostra confirmasse donationem illam quam Gilbertus Episcopus Katannie fecit Ricardo fratri suo de tota terra sua de Suthyrland. quam Hugo Fresekyn dicto Episcopo dedit. Scilicet de tota terra de SKELLEBOLLE et de Ferinbeildyn et preterea de tota terra que jacet inter dictas terras de SKELLEBOLLE et Ferinbeildyn et divisas de Ros versus occidentem. Tenendis eidem Ricardo et heredibus suis de heredibus predicti Hugonis Fresekin in feodo et hereditate per rectas divisas suas et cum omnibus justis pertinentiis suis ita libere et quiete, plenarie, et honorifice sicut carta dicti G. episcopi inde plenius confecta predicto Ricardo, et carta prenominati Hugonis Fresekyn et confirmatio domini Regis Willielmi, patris nostri super dictis terris præfato Gilberto Episcopo plenius confecte, juste testantur et confirmant. Salvo servitio nostro. Testibus, Willielmo Episcopo Glasguensi, Cancellario, P. Comite de Dunbar, Waltero filio Alani senescalli, Justiciario Scocie, Waltero Olifard, Justiciario Laodonie, Alano Hostiario, Waltero Byset, Willielmo de Mar, apud Sanctum Andream vicessimo sexto die Decembris anno regni Domini Regis vicessimo secundo.

Differences having arisen as to the construction of these several Grants in favour of the Church, it was agreed to settle the same by the following :

A.D. 1275, x. Kal. Oct.

Agreement between William Earl of Sutherland and Archibald Bishop of Caithness.

Omnibus sancte Matris ecclesie filiis, hoc scriptum visuris, vel audituris, Archibaldus miseratione divina Episcopus Cathannie, SALUTEM eternam in Domino. Cum diutina controversia quondam exorta fuit inter venerabiles patres predecessores nostros Gilebertum, Willielmum, et Walterum bone memorie Episcopos Cathannie nomine dicte ecclesie ex una parte, et Nobiles viros Willielmum clare memorie, et Willielmum ejus filium, comites Sutherlandie super castro de Schythebolle cum quibusdem aliis terris videlicet sex davatis terre de Schythebolle, et sex davatis de Syttheraw, cum passagio, et duabus davatis terre cum dimidia de Miggewet, Swerdildale, Creych, cum piscaria de le Bunnach, de Cuttheldawach, de duabus davatis de Monimor, de duabus davatis de Awelec, de tribus davatis de Promsy, de una davata de Roweherchar, de tribus quarteriis de Haskeldale, de dimidia davata de Hacchencossy, de tribus davatis de Thorebolle, de duabus davatis de Kynalde, et de quatuor davatis de Largge. In quibus terris et castro dicti predecessores nostri, nomine ecclesie Cathannie, jus sibi vendicabant a predictis Comitibus, et dicta controversia in non modicum dispendium ecclesie Cathannie, et graves sumptus dictorum Comitum diu fuit agitata et prelata usque ad tempus nostrum, et Willielmi filii predicti Comitis clare memorie ; Tandem viri fideles, et pacis zelatores prelati ecclesiarum, nobiles viri, comites et barones, et alii quem plures fidedigni, pressuris et angustiis ecclesie Cathannie, et laboribus et expensis predictorum comitum compacientes, zelo caritatis instincti, partes suas diligenter interposuerunt, ut pacem et unitatem inter ecclesiam Cathannie nos et successores nostros, et predictum nobilem Willielmum comitem, et ejus heredes, ordinarent, et in perpetuum stabilirent ; Tandem, post multas ordinaciones et prelocuciones, dictus comes consilio dictorum prelatorum, procerum et aliorum fidedignorum inclinatus, mera voluntate sua et spontanea concessit Ecclesie Cathannie, nobis et successoribus nostris.

Castrum de Schythebolle, cum 6 davatis terre adjacentibus. et

Sex Davatas terre de Sytheraw, cum passagio, et

duabus davatis cum dimidia de Miggeweth, Swerdel, et de Creych, cum piscatura de le Bunnach, et

duabus davatis de Mouimor, cum eorum pertinenciis,

Tenendas et habendas et in perpetuum pacifice possidendas ecclesie Cathannie, nobis et successoribus nostris, salvo forinseco servitio domini Regis sine aliqua controversia de cetero motura ab ipse comite vel heredibus suis,

Residue vero terre, videlicet :—

Due davate de Awelech.

Tres davate de Promsy.

Una davata de Rucherhard.

Tres quarterie de Halkesdale.

Dimidia davate de Hachencosse.

Tres davate de Thorebol.

Due davate de Kynalde.

Quatuor davate de Largge, et

Una davata de Cutheldawach.

de mera voluntate nostra, et consensu capituli nostri, residebunt penes predictum Comitem et heredes suos in perpetuum plenarie hereditarie et pacifice sine contradictione vel inquietatione moturis a nobis vel successoribus nostris. Ad hoc vero ut ecclesie nostre nobis et successoribus nostris securius esse provisum, et ut plenariam possessionem dictarum terrarum ecclesie nostre nobis et successoribus nostris a dicto Comite concessarum poterimus nancissi. Et pro utilitate et commodo nobis et successoribus nostris á dicto Comite collatis, de voluntate et consensu capituli nostri dedimus et concessimus predicto comiti, et heredibus suis unam davatam de Owenes, valentem dimidiam marcam, et quod dictus comes et sui heredes possint nobis et successoribus nostris, qui pro tempore fuerint, unum capellanum presentare, qui in perpetuum celebrabit in ecclesia de Durnach, ad altare sancti Jacobi, pro animabus dicti comitis, et predecessorum et successorum suorum, quem quidem capellanum nos et successores nostri ad presentationem predicti comitis, et heredum suorum admittemus et dicto capellano ad ejus sustentationem, quinque marcas annuas de bonis Episcopalibus, videlicet, de firmis nostris de villa nostra de Durnach per manus balivorum nostrorum, qui pro tempore fuerint, et successorum nostrorum, ad duos anni terminos videlicet ad festum Sancti Martini in yeme duas marcas cum dimidia et duas marcas cum dimidia ad pentecostes in perpetuum administrabimus: promisimus etiam de voluntate et consensu capituli nostri pro nobis et successoribus nostris, quod nos providebimus faciemus predicto comiti et ejus heredibus, omnem securitatem ad istas ordinaciones et concessiones in perpetuum inviolabiliter observandas, quam ipse et consilium suum velint et poterint de jure ordinare vel petere Et ad istam ordinacionem seu composicionem inviolabiliter in perpetuum observandam, in omnibus et per omnia prout superius scriptum est, tam nos pro nobis et successoribus nostris, tam decanus, archidiacanus, precentor, et cancellarius pro se et Capitulo Cathannie Comes pro se et heredibus suis, fidem dedimus corporalem. In cujus rei testimonium, et ad majorem hujus rei securitatem huic scripto penes comitem et ejus heredes residenti, sigillum nostrum una cum communi sigillo capituli Cathannie, et sigillo decani, archdiaconi, precentoris, et cancellarii Cathannie est appensum; Consimili vero scripture penes nos et successores nostros et Capitulum nostrum residenti, sigillum predicti comitis una cum sigillo domini Willielmo de Monte Alto, domini Andree de Moravia, domini Alexandri de Moravia, et domini David de Ynverlunan est appensum. Actum in Cathedrali ecclesia Cathannie X Kalend. Octobris Anno Gracie M.CC. Septuagesimo quinto.

A.D. 1333.

· An Indenture between Reynald Moray, son of Allan Moray of Cubin, and Kenneth Erle of Sutherland, for settling several disputes about the lands of Skelbo, and for contracting a marriage between Eustache, daughter of the said Erle, and Gilbert Moray, son of the said Reynald.

A.D. 1440.

Precept of sasine in favour of Thomas Kynnaird of that ilk, and of Egidia de Moravia of Culbin his wife, daughter and heiress of Walter de Moravia de Skelbo.

By this marriage, on the failure of the heirs male of Richard de Moravia in the direct line, Skelbo passed into the family of Kynnaird of that ilk.

A.D. 1515.

Charter by Andrew Kinnaird of that ilk, and Skelbo, in favour of John Mackay, of the lands of Edderachilis, part of the Barony of Skelbo.

A.D. 1525, July 13.

Precept of sasine by Adam Gordon, Earl of Sutherland, in favour of John Kynnard of that ilk, of the lands of

Skelbo, with the Castle and Manor place of the same:
Easter Skelbo.
Dawauchdow.
Achandra.
Paitamayne.
Balnobraid.
Cammesseffe.
Abbirschoir, Estir.
Abbirschoir, Westir.
Little Roart.
Knok Cartnall.
Moirenich.
Auchendowch.
Innirshyn, and fishings thereof.
Pittentraill.
Assent,
Artriquhillis.
With the whole Lordship of Skelbo.

A.D. 1529.

Charter by John Kynnaird of Skelbo and Kynnaird, in favour of William Sutherland, of Duffus and Thorboll, of the lands and Barony of Skelbo and its pertinents, to be holden of Alexander, Earl of Sutherland and his heirs.

IV.—BARONY OF THORBOLL.

A.D. 1360.

Charter by William (3) Earl of Sutherland in favour of his brother, Nicolas Sutherland of Duffus, comprising sexdecim davatas trē jacentes infra comitatum de Sothyrland in libera baronia que dicitur Thorbol, viz. :—

tres davatas de Thorbol
unam davatam de Rouearkar
unam davatam de Assastel
unam davatam de Proncey superiori
unam davatam de Proncey inferiori
unam davatam de Proncey croey
duas davatas de Evelek
unam davatam de Grodybrorak
unam davatam de Sibyrsoc
duas davatas de Kylpedre majori et minori
unam quarteriam de Meyngferry
unam davatam ditto
unam davatam de Cawyn jacentem ex orientali p^{te} aque de Strathully
unam davatam de Kylpedre jacentem ex orientali p^{te} aque ejusdem

Hiis Testibus Johanne Moraven. et Thoma Cathenen. dei gratia Episcopis, Thoma de Moravia panetario Scocie cum multis aliis.

A.D. 1364, Oct. 17.

Charter of Confirmation by David King of Scots.

V.—BARONY OF SKELBO AND THORBOLL.
A.D. 1560. Oct. 31.

Instrument of Sasine in favour of Alexander Sutherland of Duffus on Charter by John Earl of Sutherland with consent of Helen Countess of Errol and Sutherland, his spouse, of all and whole the Barony of Skelbo, viz.

Castelton of Skelbo, with the tower and fortalice thereof
Balvraid
Cambusavye
Ester Skelbo
Cowll
Petmayne
Miln of Skelbo
Wester Aberscors
Morynche
Roart beg
Morimor
Cragye
Auchendowyche, with the salmon fishings of the water of Innerschyn, with the lynn of the same
The lands of Innerschyn
Milns of Innerschyn

And also the Lands and Barony of

Pronsie, viz. Pronsie Casteltown, with the tower, and fortalice of the same
Pronsie nane
Proncy croye
Assidaell
Cornamanan
Rewarchar
Evelik, with the mill thereof
Dalnamayne
Mekill Torboll
Litill Torboll
Grudebrora
Syberskors
Kilpedder moir
Kilpedder beig
Mill of Kilpeddermoir
Kilpedder in Strathulzie
Cayane in Strathulzie

All lying in the Earldom of Sutherland and Sherifdom of Innerness.

A.D. 1563, June 22.

Charter under the Great Seal of Mary Queen of Scots in favour
of Alexander Sutherland Duffus, of Skelbo, Thorboll, and Proncy,
of all and whole the lands hereinbefore described in the Sasine
dated Oct. 31, 1560.

A.D. 1787.

Charter in favour of Alexander Mackenzie, W.S., as trustee for
the Marchioness of Stafford of the Barony of Assynt, and others,
proceeding on a decree decreet of Sale against James (Sutherland)
Lord Duffus.

A.D. 1804, May 14.

Disposition by A. Mackenzie in favour of the Marchioness of
Stafford, viz. of all and whole the Town Lands and Barony of
Skelbo, with the castle, tower, fortalice, and Manor place of Skelbo

The town and lands of

Easter Skelbo
Coull
Gallutter
Crockgrass
Middle Skelbo
Auchendren
Cubay
Balvraid

As also the haill Town and Lands of

Grudie
Pitgrudie
Braegrudie
Craigie
Carroch more ⎫
Kurinamain ⎬
Langwell ⎭
Wester Aberscross
Easter Aberscross
Muckle Torboll and Mill Lands thereof
Little Torboll

Dalnamain and brae thereof
Auchenduich
Invershin
Meikle Balblair

The Town and Lands of
Evelichs, the Mill thereof
The Town and Lands of
Pronsie Castle
Pronsie
Pronsie croy
Pronsie nain
Nether Pronsie
Kinnauld

Town and Lands of
Blairisk, and mill thereof
Town and Lands of
Sciberscross
Aliemoile
Little Rogart
Knock Arthur
Moriness
Morvich
Pittentrail
Pitfuir
Blairich
Leadie
Carry and Kilfedder
Rearquhar
Auchnosnich and
Ausdale
Auchincoich
Meikle Balblair
Balchraggan
with all castles, &c.

A. D. 1807.

Disposition by the Marquis and Marchioness of Stafford in
favour of themselves of the Lands and Barony above mentioned.

VI.—ASSYNT.

Assynt remained in the Skelbo titles until 1525, but it was
possessed by the Macleods and afterwards by the
Mackenzies, until March 2nd, 1696.

A. D. 1696, March 2.

Disposition by Countess Dowager of Seaforth in favour of John
Mackenzie of Assynt of all and whole the lands and baronies of
Assynt, comprehending the towns and lands following :—

Assin,
Elvin,
Auldinachie,
Knockan,
Cromald,
Inverkirkaike,
Culaick,
Knockanmuaich,
Tubegg,
Assinbegg,
Loch Bennoch,
Dowghlich,
Drumswarcallen
Sulvine,
Inverbaddie,
Darrach,
Torbreck,
Aldrow,
Auchinalnich,
Claichtoktovie
Clashmore,
Achincairine,
Clasness,
Aldenhie,
Drumback,
Nadde,
Glenreaeh,
Ardmore,
Kintraide,

Ulladill,

Achmore,

Ardvrach,

Achnaheglaishe,

Inschnauld,

Stroncubry,

Laun,

Leadowbegg,

Leadowmore,

as also the Milnes of Assin, and of the Towns, Lands, and others foresaid, and with all and sundry Lochs, Rivers, and Waters belonging to the said lands, and particularly the water

Inver,

Invercoulaick,

Inverkirkaick,

with the Salmon and other fishings great and small, and pertinents therein more particularly described, and the Tower, Fortalice and Manor Places respective of Assin, to be holden of the Countess of Seaforth as superior thereof, together with the advocation, donation, and right of Patronage of the Kirk and parish of Assynt, Chapelainries, Prebendaries and Tiends, Parsonage and Vicarage of the same, and also the heritable office of Bailliary of the Barony of Assin.

A.D. 1757, July 21.

Decree of Sale of the Lands and Barony or reputed Barony of Assynt, part of the Barony of Skelbo in favour of Catharine Lady Strathnaver, on disposition of Kenneth Mackenzie, comprehending the towns and lands underwritten, videlicet:

Glenlerack,

Nedd,

Trumpack,

Culkan,

Ulbonny,

Unapull,

Cromald,

Auldneachie,

Elphin,

Knockan,
Leadbegg, and Miln thereof;
Leadmore,
Riencruch,
Stronchrubie,
Douchlash,
Drumswardalen,
Knokineach,
Inverkirkhag,
Culachs,
Fillin,
Inver,
Badidarroch,
Airdraw,
Torbreck,
Assint beg,
Lochbainish,
Auchincloish,
Clashmore,
Brachlishe,
Oldinnie, and
Islands of Ellandura, and
Ellanchrona,
Stoir,
Clachtoll,
Clashneshie, and Miln thereof;
Auchnacarnan,
Ardvair,
Rientrade,
Auchmore, with
Tuimoir and Poulheargain,
Cullen,
Camore,
Two Tubeggs,
Inchnadampf,
Edrachalda, and Mill thereof;
and all other Towns and Mountains, Valleys, &c., and the
   Advocation, Donation, and right of Patronage of the Kirk
   and Parish of Assint, and all chaplaincries, &c.

VII.—DILRID AND STRATHNAVER.

A.D. 1370.

Disposition by John (1) Earl of Sutherland, in favour of Hector
Sutherland, his second son, of Dilrid and other lands in Sutherland and Caithness.

See Sir Robert Gordon, p. 55, and the Sutherland additional
case.

A.D. 1495, Oct. 2.

Decree by Lords of Session on the complaint of Margaret Baillie,
Countess-Dowager of Sutherland, wife of Alexander Dumbar,
against Sir James Dumbar, her brother-in-law, and John Rioch
Mackay *in* Strathnaver, for impeding her in the peaceable possession of her lands of Crakok, Loth, Colnagour, and one-third
of the lands of —— Sextounis.

Sutherland of Dilrid, having killed the said Alexander Dumbar,
for comprising some of his lands for debt; he was outlawed by
JAMES IV. who promised to bestow his lands on whoever would
deliver him up to justice, which service was performed by his,
Dilrid's uncle, Y Roy Mackay IN Strathnaver, upon which the
King conferred on him by the following

A D. 1499, Nov. 4.

Disposition of James IV. of the lands undermentioned to Y
Makkie.

Jacobus IV. Dei gratia Rex Scotorum omnibus probis hominibus
totius terræ suæ clericis laicis salutem, Sciatis nos pro bono fideli
et gratuito servitio nobis per dilectum servitorem nostrum Odonem
alias Y Makky *in* Strathnavern, tam tempore pacis quam guerre
impenso et impendendo et signaliter in captione et asportatione
nobis quondam Alexandrum Sutherland de Dilrid, et aliarum
decem personarum ejus complicium nostrorum Rebellium et ad
nostrum Cornŭ existen. dedisse, concessisse et hac presenti carta
nostra confirmasse, dicto Odoni Makki et heredibus suis omnes et
singulas terras subscriptas, viz. : terras de

Fer	Dylrid
Armidill	Cattack

Strae	Bronach
Rynivee	Killchalmkill in Strathbroray
Kynald	Davach, Loch Naver
Gollesby	Davach, Erebull

et duas denariatas terrarum de Stromay cum molendino de Kynnald cum suis pertinen. jacen. in Caithness et Sutherland infra Comitatum nostrum de Innerness. Quæ quidem terræ et molendinum cum suis pertinent. fuerunt dicti quond. Alexandri Sutherland hereditarie et nunc nobis pertinent, et in manibus nostris legitime devenerunt ratione forisfacture per justificationem dicti quond. Alexandri de proditoria traditione convicti. Tenend. et habend. omnes et singulas predictas terras de Fer, &c.—Dicto Odoni alias Y Makky, et heredibus suis de nobis et successoribus nostris in feodo et hereditate in perpetuum per omnes rectas metas suas antiquas prout jacent. in longitudine et latitudine, &c. Reddendo annuatim dictus Odo Makky et hæredes sui nobis et successoribus nostris pro predict: terris et molendinis cum pertinent. unam roseam rubeam in festo nativitatis beati Joannis Baptiste supra solum predictarum terrarum de Dilrid nomine albæ firmæ si petatur tantum. In cujus rei testimonium presenti cartæ nostræ magnum sigillum nostrum appendi percepimus, &c. &c.

Apud Innerness 4º die mensis Novembris, 1499, et regni nostri duodecimo.

After this date, the family of Mackay are generally styled *of* Strathnaver, having been previously styled Mackays *in* Strathnaver.

A.D. 1551.

The lands included in the said Charter of 1499, were forfeited to the Crown on the illegitimacy of the children of Y Roy Mackay. (See Sir Robert Gordon, p. 155.) Mackay.

A.D. 1563.

Charter by Queen Mary on her coming of age, in favour of the Earl of Huntley, of the said lands included in the Charter of 1499.

A.D. 1570.

Charter by the Earl of Huntley of the dominium Utile of these lands to Hucheon Mackay.

A.D. 1583.

Disposition by the Earl of Huntley, in favour of (1) Alexander Earl of Sutherland of the superiority of the lands in the Charter of 1499, in exchange for the Lordship of Aboyne.

A.D. 1630.

Disposition by Sir Robert Gordon, in favour of John (6) Earl of Sutherland, of Golspietower, which he had purchased from Mackay.

A.D. 1642.

Charter by Donald, first Lord Reay, in favour of John, Earl of Sutherland, of the Lordship of
    Strathnaver.

VIII.—UPPAT.

A.D. 1812, March 30.

Disposition by William Munro of Achany in favour of the Marquis of Stafford of the town and mains of
    Uppat, with the pendicles of
    Strathsteven, and
    Sputhri.

IX.—CARROL, ETC.

A.D. 1812, July 23.

Disposition by Joseph Gordon and consent of others in favour of the Marquis of Stafford of
    Kilnabraren,
    Carrole,
    Killicallumkill, and mills thereof.

X.—ARMADALE, STRATHY, PORTSKERRA.

A.D. 1813, Feb. 19.

Disposition by the Trustees of Lord Armadale in favour of the Marquis of Stafford of the town and lands of

Strathy, with the grazings of

Mellantea,

Baddandow,

Kearloch,

Strathy Kearloch,

Spellach,

Toranascray,

Baddy and Loanaclach, with the salmon fishings in the water of Strathy,

Balblair,

Gairsarg,

Strathyhead,

Auldermohr,

Baligill,

Miltown, with mill thereof,

Dalvait,

Daldibagg, and mill thereof,

Dalterie,

Bowside,

Dallangwell,

Bracrathy.

All and haill the town and lands of Armadale, with the pendicles of

Istrumen,

Auldiport,

Brawlmill of Armadale. All and haill the lands of Portskerray,

Halladale, with salmon fishings thereof.

I

XI.—LINSITMORE, ETC.

A.D. 1824, Oct. 1.

Disposition by R. A. Macleod of Cadboll, in favour of the
Marquis of Stafford, all and whole the town and lands of
Inveran, and mill thereof, and the pertinents of the
said lands, viz. :

Glenshinn, with the woods thereof,

Garvald,

Tinald. And the town and lands of

Linsitcroy,

Linsitmore, and the woods thereof, with the pendicle
of

Duchelly.

XII.—REAY COUNTRY.

A.D. 1829, May 13.

Disposition by Eric Lord Reay in favour of the Marquis of
Stafford, of the Reay Country, to be held of the Marchioness
of Stafford, as Countess of Sutherland.

*Charter of Confirmation by the Marchioness of Stafford and
Countess of Sutherland; in favour of the Marquis of Stafford
of the Reay Country.*

A.D. 1830.

To all and sundry to whose knowledge these presents shall
come, I, Elizabeth Marchioness of Stafford and Countess of
Sutherland, immediate lawful superior of the lands and others
underwritten, with the special advice and consent of the most
noble George Granville Marquis of the County of Stafford, my
husband, and I, the said Marquis, for myself, my own right and
interest, and we both with one consent Greeting, KNOW YE that I
have with consent foresaid RATIFIED, APPROVED, and perpetually

CONFIRMED, like as I the said Marchioness and Countess with consent foresaid, do hereby RATIFY, APPROVE, and for me, my heirs and successors perpetually, CONFIRM to and in favour of my LOVITE the said GEORGE GRANVILLE, Marquis of the County of Stafford, his heirs and assignees whatsoever heritably and irredeemably, a disposition dated the fifteenth day May, One thousand eight hundred and twenty-nine, and registered in the Books of Council and Session the second day of June, thereafter made and granted by the Right Honorable Eric Lord Reay, whereby the said Eric Lord Reay for the causes therein specified, SOLD, ALIENATED, and DISPONED to, and in favour of the said George Granville, Marquis of the County of Stafford, his heirs and assignees whatsoever heritably and irredeemably, all and sundry the lands, milns, fishings, teind sheaves, and others after specified, comprehending and constituting the whole Estate and Country of Reay, and the whole of the lands and heritages belonging to the said Eric Lord Reay, lying in the County of Sutherland or in the County of Caithness as hereafter mentioned, viz.:

All and haill the town and lands of
Ribigill Miln, and miln lands thereof,
Keanlochmore,
Keanlochbeg,
Mussal,
Dalkeapach,
Ylandryer,
Arnaboll, and the salmon fishings upon the water of
    Drietary Hunloum,
Miln, and Miln lands thereof,
Eriboll,
Strathbeg,
Ylandchoirie,
Houp, and salmon fishings thereof.
The Forest and Forest lands of Diriemore, and
Forest towns of Auldinnie,
Loane, and salmon fishings thereof upon the water of
    Garnrone,
Ardbeg,
Ardmore,
Keanlochbervie,

Alschourbeg,
Alschourmore,
Carumanoch,
Sandwood,
Kearvag,
Havish,
Keoldale, and salmon fishings in the water of Duirness and
    Cruives thereof,
Crangillicle,
Borlie,
Slamaness,
Balnakill,
Forret,
Gavel,
Crossbell,
Balnamulich,
Sandgayes,
Ylandhoan,
Rispyne,
Fraskill,
Strathmelness,
Melness,
Milns, and Miln lands of the same,
Ylandgyle,
Scorlumy,
Strathtongue,
Caldabachlie,
Tongue,
Miln, and Miln lands thereof,
Kirkaboll,
Scrabuster,
Kinnesaide,
Releyden,
Oldlangwart,
Torrantarrow,
Lettermore,
Borgiemore,
Torrisdale,

Skerra,

Ylandroyan,

Ylandcolme,

All and haill the lands of

Ederachilles, with the pertinents thereof, viz.:

Fenziedailles,

Laxfurd, with salmon fishings of the same,

Scouribeg,

Scouriemore,

Cauldstroam,

Handa Island,

With the teind sheaves of all and sundry the foresaid lands and Barony of ARDURNESS pertaining and belonging thereto, viz.: of all and haill the lands of

Galdwall,

Kealdale,

Cramugacle,

Gerrongarve,

Terragawish,

Carnmanoch,

Borly,

Slaness,

Salmon fishings upon the water of Avongarrone, and Sandwood, and

Salmon fishings upon the water of Ardurness,

And the fishing of cruives thereof whatsoever, with the mill and multures of the same, as also the island of HOA and other islands there, with the seaports of all and sundry the lands and others above written, and all other fishings of the same, as well in fresh as in salt waters, as also of the lands of

Sandwood,

Alschourbeg,

Alschourmore,

with all and sundry towers, fortalices, manor places, houses, biggings, yards, orchyards, milns, woods, fishings, outsetts, insetts, annexis connexis, dependencies, shealings, pastures, tenants, tenandries, and services of free tenants, parts, pendicles, privileges, and pertinents of the same, whatsoever and sick like.

All and whole the towns, lands, and Barony of FARR, comprehending the towns and lands after mentioned, viz. :

Armadale,

Strathy, with the salmon fishings thereof,

Strathhaladale, comprehending

Galdwall,

Balnahyglash, with the salmon fishings of the same, as also the lands of

Bronach,

Delrit,

Cattach,

lying within the Diocese and Sheriffdoms of Caithness and Sutherland, with all and sundry parts, pendicles, and pertinents thereof, Declaring that the said Barony of Farr does not extend to nor comprehend the lands of

Golspitour,

Kinauld,

Ikolmkiln,

Instrathbrora,

Lochnaver,

Strathnaver, the salmon fishings upon the water of Naver,

Farr,

Kirktomie,

with the miln and pertinents thereof, which were disponed in property by George Lord Reay, or his father, grandfather, or great grandfather to John Earl of Sutherland, his predecessors or authors, if any such were, together with all other lands and heritages, if any be, belonging to the said Eric Lord Reay, lying within the County of Sutherland or in the County of Caithness, whether therein named or not named, and all right, title and interest, claim of right, property and possession, petitory or possessory, which he, his predecessors or authors, heirs or successors, had, have, or could any way claim to the lands, baronies, and others above written, or any part or portion thereof, or to any annual rents or yearly duties upliftable forth of the same, AND THAT in the whole heads, articles, clauses, tenor and contents thereof, with the obligement to infeft a me vel de me percept of sasine and other clauses therein contained, together with the instrument of sasine following thereon in favour of the said George Granville, Marquis of the County of Stafford, dated the eighteenth, nineteenth, twentieth, twenty-second, twenty-third, twenty-fourth, and twenty-fifth days of June, One thousand eight hundred and twenty-nine, and registered in the General Register of Sasines kept at Edinburgh, the thirteenth day of July, there after in the whole heads, articles, clauses, tenor and contents thereof, with all that has followed or may follow thereupon. And I, the said Elizabeth Marchioness of Stafford and Countess of Sutherland, with consent foresaid, WILL and GRANT, and for myself, my heirs and successors, DECERN and ORDAIN that this present Confirmation is and shall be as valid and sufficient, and of as great force strength and effect to all intents and purposes as if the writs before confirmed had been verbatim engrossed herein, or as if the present confirmation had been made and granted before the taking of the said infeftment, WHEREANENT and with all other objections, defects and imperfections, which may be proponed against the validity of the said writs hereby confirmed, or this present confirmation thereof, I have dispensed and by these presents, with consent aforesaid, DISPENSE for ever. To BE HOLDEN the said several towns, lands, and others before described, as follows : the said towns and lands of Ribigill Miln, and Miln Lands thereof, Keanlochmore, Keanlochbeg, Mussal, Dalkessock, Ylandryer, Arnaboll, and the salmon fishings on the water of Drydarg, and Hunloun, Miln, and Miln Lands thereof, Eriboll, Strathbeg, Ylandchoirie, Houp, and the salmon fishings thereof, the Forest and Forest lands of Diriemore, Keanlochbervie, Fraskill, Strathmelness, Melness Miln, and miln lands thereof, Ylandgyle, Scorlumy and Strathtongue, Coldaballe, Tongue, Miln and miln lands thereof, Kirkabull, Scrabuster, Kinnisaide, Releyden, Old Langwart, Torrantarrow, Lettermore, Farr, Miln, and miln lands thereof, Kirktomie, Borgiemore, Torrisdale, Skerra, Ylandroan, Ylandcolme, and the foresaid lands of EDERACHILLES, with the pertinents, viz.; the lands of Fenziedailles and Laxfurd, with the salmon fishings thereof; Scouriebeg, and Scouriemore, Caldstrone and island of Handa and the foresaid lands and BARONY OF FARR, comprehending the lands and others above written, which were formerly held of me, the said Marchioness and Countess and my predecessors in taxt

ward for yearly payment of ten merks Scots money for the ward
and the like sum of ten merks money foresaid for the marriage,
are now holden of me the said Marchioness and Countess in feu
farm, by virtue of the Act of Parliament of the twentieth year of
his Majesty King George the Second, entituled, " An Act for
taking away the tenure of ward holdings in Scotland, and for
converting the same into feu and blench holdings." And the
said lands before and after mentioned of the BARONY OF ARDUR-
NESS and teind sheaves of the same, which were formerly held of
me, the said Marchioness and Countess, and my predecessors in
feu, with clauses de non alienando for payment of the feuduty
after mentioned and performances of the personal services of
hosting and attending me the said Marchioness and Countess, my
predecessors in all Parliaments to be held in Scotland, now of me,
my heirs and successors in simple feu by virtue of the Act of
Parliament of his Majesty, King George the First, entitled,
"An Act for more effectually securing the peace of the High-
lands of Scotland," and by virtue of the other Act of Parliament
above mentioned. And all and sundry the lands, milns, fishings,
teinds, and others above mentioned, are now holden of me the
said Marchioness and Countess, my heirs and successors, in feu
farm and heritage ; GIVING therefor yearly the said George Granville, Marquis of the County of Stafford and his foresaids, to me
the said Elizabeth Marchioness of Stafford and Countess of
Sutherland, and my heirs and successors, the feu farm duties and
others underwritten. To wit for the foresaid lands of RIBIGILL
and others before expressed, which were formerly held, taxed
ward, the sum of five shillings and four pennies Scots money, in
name of feu farm duty, and freeing me the said Marchioness and
Countess, and my heirs of the yearly duties and other debts of
feu farm money, if any such be payable or demandable by
any person forth of the foresaid lands of Ribigill, Sandwood, Island of Hoa, Aschourbeg, and Aschourmore, and also
freeing and relieving me, the said Marchioness and Countess, and
my heirs of all taxations imposed or to be imposed by our Sovereign Lord the King, on the foresaid lands, and that for all other
burden, exaction, demand, or secular service that may be exacted
or required forth of the lands, fishings, and others foresaid in any
manner of way. And for the foresaid fishings on the water of Garn-

rone, Ardbeg, Ardmore, Aschourmore, Aschourbeg, Carumanoch, Sandwood, Kearvag, Havish, Kealdale and salmon fishings upon the water of Duirness, and cruives thereof; Cromgillicle, Borlie, Slamanis, Balnakiel, Forret, Gavell, Crossbell, Balnamulick, Sandgaves, Ylandhoan, Rispyne, the sum of Eighty-four pounds Scots money, at the term of Martinmas yearly, as the ancient feu duty, payable out of the same, and of the further sum of Twenty-four pounds Scots money of feu duty at the term of Martinmas, yearly, as the value and in lieu of the personal services before mentioned, and of the clauses de non alienando, wherewith the Investitures of the foresaid BARONY OF DURNESS, and teinds of the same were formerly burdened, and DOUBLING the foresaid sums of Eighty-four pounds and Twenty-four pounds Scots, the first year of the Entry of each Heir to the foresaid Lands and Teinds, and relieving me, the said Marchioness and Countess, my heirs and successors, of the sum of Forty shillings Scots money, which we are bound to pay to our Sovereign Lord the King for the forsaid Lands and Teinds of the forsaid Lands and Barony of AR-DURNESS, yearly at two terms in the year, Whitsunday, and Martinmas in Winter, by equal portions, and Sicklike, freeing and relieving me, the said Marchioness and Countess, my heirs and successors of all ministers' stipends, annual rents, burdens, and taxes imposed or to be imposed upon the foresaid fishings on the water of Garnrone, lands of Ardbeg, Ardmore, and other lands and fishings aforesaid, for which the said sums of Eighty-four pounds and Twenty-four pounds of feu duty are payable and on the aforesaid Teinds, Sheaves of the Lands and Barony of Ardurness, and with power and liberty to me, the said Marchioness and Countess, and my heirs and successors of hunting once every year in the foresaid forest of Diriemore and Durness, without any stop or impediment, Sicklike as freely and with such privileges as the predecessors of the said George Granville, Marquis of the County of Stafford, have at any time bye past hunted, or the said Marquis hereafter shall hunt, within the same. As also that the said George Granville, Marquis of the County of Stafford, and his foresaids, shall be bound and obliged to accompany and attend me the said Marchioness and Countess, and my foresaids during the time of our hunting in the said forest of Diriemore and Duirness, if thereto required upon premonition of twenty-four days, and if it shall

K

happen the foresaid feu duty of One hundred and eight pounds Scots to run for two years into the third unpaid, then and in that case the said feu duty of three years shall be doubled, and if the payment of the said feu duty shall run for three years into the fourth unpaid, then and in that case this present Charter, so far as concerns the foresaid lands of the Barony of ARDURNESS and Teinds thereof with all that may follow therein, shall thenceforth become null and void, as if the same had never been granted, and that without the necessity of any other process of declaration to be raised hereupon, and that for all other burden, exaction, demand, or secular service that may be any ways exacted or required forth of the towns, lands, islands, waters, fishings, and teind sheaves aforesaid, saving always and reserving my own right and the right of all others, as accords of the law. And I consent to the registration thereof in the Books of Council and Session, therein to remain for preservation, and to that effect I constitute, &c.

MELNESS, HOPE, &c.

A.D. Sept. 4, 1379.

Charter of Confirmation under the Great Seal by Robert II. to Ferchard his physician.

Robertus Dei Gratia Rex Scotorum omnibus probis hominibus totius terre sue Salutem Sciatis nos approbasse ratificasse et hac presenti Carta nostra confirmasse donationem illam et concessionem quam dilectus filius noster Alexander Senechallus miles dominus de Badenach fecit et concessit Ffercardo medico nostro de terris de Melness et de duabus partibus de Hoip cum pertinenciis, Tenend. et habend. dicto Ffercardo cum omnibus singulis libertatibus, commoditatibus aysiamentis et justis pertinentiis spectantibus seu quoque modo juste spectaturis, valentibus in futurum adeo libere et quiete, plenarie, integre et honorifice, in omnibus et per omnes sicut Carta dicti filii nostri eodem medico exinde confecta plenius inde continet. et prof. salvo servicio nostro. In cujus rei testimonium presenti Carte nostre nostrum precipimus apponi sigillum Testibus Venerabilibus in Christo patribus, Willielmo et Johanne Cancellario nostro ecclesiarum sancti Andree et Dun-

keldensis Episcopis — Johanne primogenito nostro de Carric
Seneschalio Scotie.—Roberto de Ffyffe et de Menteth filio nostro
delecto.—Willielmo de Douglas   de Mar consanguineo
nostro Comitibus Jacobo de Lyndsay nepote nostro carissimo
et Alexandro Consanguineo nostro militibus et Alexandro de
Lyndesay apud Perthe quarto die mensis Septembri et anno regni
nostri nono.

Charter of Robert II. in favour of Ferchard Lieche.

A.D. 1386, Dec. 31.

Robertus dei gratia Rex Scotorum omnibus probis hominibus
totius terre sue clericis et laycis Salutem, Sciatis nos dedisse, concessisse et hac presente nostra carta nostra confirmasse dilecto et
fideli nostro Fferchardo Lecke pro suo servitio nobis facto et
faciendo Insulas de Jura (now Oldeney, see process in Dunrobin
Charter-room ;)

Sanda, necnon et ;
Elangawne,
Elanewillighe,
Elancrone,
Elane hoga,
Elaneqwhochra,
Elanegelye,
Elaneuyofo, et omnes insulas nostras jacentes inter ;
Rowestorewastynghe, et
Row Armedale, infra

Vicecomitatum de Innȳs. Tenend. et habend. eidem Ffercardo,
et heredibus suis de nobis et heredibus nostris in feodo hereditate
per suas rectas metas et divisas cum omnibus singulis libertatibus
comoditatibus aysiamentis et justis pertinentiis quiscunq. ad easdem
insulas pertinentibus seu pertinere valentibus in futurum libere
quiete plenarie integre et honorifice bene et in pace faciendo nobis
et heredibus nostris dictus Ffercardus et heredes sui servitia anti-
quitus inde debita et consueta in cujus rei testimonium presenti
carte nostre nostrum precipimus apponi Sigillum Reverendissimo
in Christo patre Waltero Dei Gratia sedis apostolice Cardinali,
Venerabili in Christo patre Joanne Episcopo Dunkelden, Can-

cellario nostro. Joanne primogenito nostro de Carric Seneschallo Scotie. Robertos de Ffyffe et de Mouteith. Jacobo de Douglas filiis nostris dilectis Comitibus Archibaldo de Douglas et Thoma de Erskyne Consanguineis nostris militibus. Apud Edinburgh ultimo die Decembri anno regni nostri Sexto decimo.

A.D. 1511.

Resignation by Donald Macourchie of lands in Milness and Hope, as the descendant of Farquhar Leiche to the King, in favour of Eye McKy and his son.

Note—This Ferchard or Farquhar is thus noticed in the original Statistical Account of Scotland, vol. vi. page 293, under the head of Edderachyllis—

" All these islands from Roe-a-Stoir in Assint to Stroma in Orkney, were granted to one Ferchard Beton, a native of Isla, a famous physician, at his own request, by one of the Stewarts, Kings of Scotland, whom he had cured of some distemper. This Ferchard was physician to the Mackays of Far, who gave him in exchange for these islands, lands near Melness, opposite Tongue —the possession of which they recovered long since, yet it is said that some of his posterity remain still (1793) in the country under the name of Mackay."*

Being desirous to learn if any such tradition still existed, I begged of the late Mr. George Taylor to ascertain how this was, when he visited Melness in the course of a Tour which he was then (1831) making.

The inquiries which he then made led to the following interesting account. He found that the name and the reputation of the physician was still known. His skill was thus accounted for— from his reading, he learnt, that if a white serpent could be caught and boiled into a liquid, the possessor of that liquid would acquire the faculty of curing all diseases; his learning warned him at the same time that the serpent must not be caught or the liquid prepared by the person who was to obtain this wonderful gift—and further, that whoever caught the serpent, and

---

* It will be seen from the foregoing Charters, that this statement is not accurate in all particulars.

prepared the liquid, was not to be informed of the object of that in which he was employed.

Ferchard accordingly placed a youth who was in his service at the place where the serpent would appear. He was instructed to touch none but the white serpent—ten serpents were allowed to issue from the hole uninjured, but the eleventh being a white one, was caught, boiled, converted into a liquid, carefully corked up in a phial, and delivered to the physician. The youth was immediately sent out of the country.

Ferchard in possession of this precious liquid made many cures.

Mr. Taylor was also informed that Ferchard was celebrated for curing the toothache by administering the juice obtained from the bark of a tree which grew in a corner of the garden at Melness, and some of the older people said that they had some recollection of the bark of a tree being used for medicinal purposes. Mr. Taylor carefully examined the garden, where no tree then grew (1831), and he discovered the remains of an old ash tree, the stringent bark of which, no doubt, was used with advantage in curing the toothache.

Having thus ascertained the prevalence of this tradition in the parish of Tongue, on the northernmost shores of Scotland, it became a question of more than ordinary curiosity to learn whether any traces of a similar tradition existed in Isla—also Ferchard's reputed birth place; which fact was established in a remarkable manner, through the kindness of Mr. Campbell of Isla, who wrote to his factor, forwarding several queries that I put into his hands. That gentleman reported to Mr. Campbell that there existed several traditions concerning Beton, the King's physician. The following is the substance of the most interesting.

He stated that the belief was, that about the year 1370 an Englishman named Cockspur having been on a visit to Isla, " was murdered through the jealousy of the chief authorities of the island," that "his servant or attendant, Duncan Beton, escaped a similar fate through the interposition of a young girl named Grant, whom he afterwards married, and by whom he had two sons, John and Duncan."

These two sons were sent to Glasgow for their education. The eldest became abbot of Mull, the second became the pupil of a celebrated Irish physician, named Olahow. While Duncan still remained in Glasgow with his master, Olahow, an Isla man visited the latter, carrying a twig in his hand—upon his being questioned why he did so and where he got it, he replied, that he had cut it in Gruimeart in Isla, on a bank named Coadan, where a white serpent was to be found. Upon which Olahow called his pupil, Duncan Beton, and directed him to proceed to the place and secure the white serpent,—which he would boil, and secure the liquor in a glass bottle—this Beton performed, but in boiling the liquid a drop being likely to escape, he pushed it back with his finger, which burned it so much, that he put it into his mouth to soothe the pain.

He returned to Glasgow with the bottle to his master, who at once declared it deficient by one drop. Beton explained how this was, upon which Olahow declared he had become master of the secret, and congratulated him on his success.

Beton immediately began his practice, and with such success, that his reputation reaching the ears of the King, he was sent for, and had the luck to cure his Majesty, who desired him to name his reward ; he said he presumed to ask the five merk lands of Monegh, Conant, now Ballinbay, which were granted to him.

The similarity of the stories handed down in these two remark-able traditions, curiously connected with legal documents, gives rise to some interesting questions as to the value of such tradi-tions. In this case they have remained perfect for near 500 years—the coincidence in point of date assigned to the arrival of Cockspur in Isla, 1370, and the date of the grant by Alexander Stewart, the Wolf of Badenoch, immediately previous to 1379, is striking. But the prevalence of such traditions for so long a period in districts so far removed from each other, having so little intercourse together during the above period, leads to the inference that they are founded upon some tradition older than either.

Is there any such tradition traceable either in Celtic or Scandi-navian story ? It has to be noticed that Duncan is the Isla, Ferchard is the northern name of Beton, and the latter, is the Charter name.

XIII.—BIGHOUSE.

A.D. 1511.

Bighouse belonged in fee simple to Murray of Spenziedale.

A.D. 1557.

Rory Murray was the first who assumed the designation of Murray of Bighouse.

A.D. 1597.

Disposition by Rory Murray in favour of William Mackay of Balnakyll, son of Y Mackay, uncle of Donald, first Lord Reay.

A.D. 1630, July 23.

Disposition by Donald Lord Reay, in favour of Angus Mackay, son of William Mackay, of Bighouse, of the lands of Golvall.

A.D. 1631, May 2.

Balnaheglish or Strathalladale, and the salmon fishings thereof.

A.D. 1830, July 23.

Charter and Resignation by Major Colin Mackay, great grandson of George Mackay, Lord Reay, in favour of the Marquis of Stafford and his heirs, and all and whole the lands of Bighouse, comprising,

> Frantle,
> Frantlemore,
> Frantlebeg. All and haill the lands of
> Forsies,
> Forsannain,
> Torsannaird,
> and the teinds, parsonages and vicarages of the said haill lands, comprehending the whole land of Upper Hallowdale, with all and sundry manor-places, castles, towers, fortalices, houses, biggings, yards, orchards, milns, miln lands, multars, and sequels of the same, mosses, moors, outsetts, insetts, shealings, woods,

groves, grasses, pasturages, commonries, privileges, pools, pendicles, and uncovered pertinents of the foresaid several towns and lands lying in Strathhalladale, within the parish of Reay, diocese of Caithness, anciently within the Sheriffdom of Inverness, and now within the Sheriffdom of Sutherland, and also all the lands of

Lower Hallowdale, with the salmon fishings of the same,
   the said lands comprehending the lands of

Kirkton,

Achoridigell,

Achow-camsaig,

Melvich,

Fors,

Torrinver,

Golwall,

Corkall,

Crachmore,

Dispollis,

Connigill,

Island Spurian,

Cluchhutagach,

Keigary,

Evachroy, with the haill pertinents thereof.

XIV.—CREICH.

A.D. 1833, July 6.

Charter and resignation of Thomas Houstoun, and others, in favour of the Marquis of Stafford.

      All and whole the town and lands of
      Creichmore,
      Creichblair,
      Rhin-funiach,
      Badercourie,
      Baderlourie,
      Carris or Camis ;
      Ledmore, with the woods of,
      Torbreck, and shealing of.

XV.—LANGWELL.

A.D. 1837, June.

Disposition by George Dempster of Skibo, in favour of the Duke of Sutherland, of the lands of
      Langwell.

Thus were the lands which were alienated in 1136, 1360, 1370, and at other times, reunited to the possessions of the Sutherland family.